MILLEDGEVILLE
TAPESTRY

Christmas love
to
David & Lisa
2008

MILLEDGEVILLE TAPESTRY

A collection of works by the
Milledgeville
Learning-In-Retirement
Writers' Group

Edited by Mary B. Purcell

Old Capital Press

Milledgeville Tapestry
©2008 Milledgeville Learning-In-Retirement Writers'
Group, respective authors

ISBN: 978-1-4357-1987-3

For more information about Old Capital Press, as well as
information about orders for this book, please visit
tllsga.org/ocp.htm

Dedication

Milledgeville Tapestry is dedicated to Colonel Lovett Briggs; it is with the deepest respect and love that we choose to honor one of our own. Lovett was, before his death in 2005, a Charter member of the Learning-in-Retirement Writers' Group and had supported our efforts to reach our goal of establishing a writers' group in Milledgeville.

His dedication to causes he believed in went back to his early days of commitment to the U.S. Military in which he served both the U.S. Navy and the U.S. Army (from which he retired in 1977). He was instrumental in establishing the American Legion Post 6 (Milledgeville) and in providing the local newspapers editorials on his beliefs in patriotism. Although born and raised near Savannah, Georgia, Lovett chose to retire and live in Milledgeville near the school he attended, Georgia Military College, which he supported faithfully.

I heard an interesting story the other day. It seems that a local school teacher had received permission from the school board to take her students on a field trip to the Museum of Aviation in Warner Robins only to be told after the trip was well underway that funds were not available. This fact came to the attention of Lovett and he went to the classroom with a check for over $500.00 to pay for the trip. The teacher was amazed. But those of us who knew him and loved him can truly say "that sounds like Lovett."

When he was facing death in 2005 in the Georgia War Veterans Home, and he had faced death before, he had friends and family who traveled great distances to encourage him and show their respect and love for a fellow human being by signing a book provided by his daughter Cherri Faith. One of those entries is by his grandson Chad Faith and it reads in part "I am not here to do anything but share a little of what you have given over the years. Thank you for showing me how to have a big heart."

All of us at Learning-in-Retirement Writers' Group share in this same thought, and we thank you, Lovett, for all you have done for us and our community.

Mary Binnicker Purcell

Acknowledgments

It is with sincere gratitude and appreciation that the Learning-in-Retirement Writers' Group presents this collection of works. Without the help and expert advice of the following, it would still be a dream. We wish to thank you and acknowledge your contributions.

Dr. Therry Dawne Nash Deal
Bill and Mary Walling
George and Jean Head
Dr. John Sallstrom
Susan Lindsley
Ken Jasnau
Ed Bzdyk
Ed Grisamore
Pam Beer, Editor, The Baldwin Bulletin
Mark Pelton and Continuing Education of GCSU
Kell Carpenter
Barry Reese
Rev. Lamar Carney and the members and staff of
  First Presbyterian Church, Milledgeville, Georgia
Dr. Dorothy Leland, President, Georgia College &
  State University

Contents

Bringing an Inanimate Object to Life
Lovett Briggs

Have you ever talked to a portrait, a photograph, or a memento that has been in the family for years? No? Well I have and still do. Mostly we talk quietly playing mind games. No one can hear us because it is all in our minds. But what we talk about is serious business. I don't talk to mementos very much mostly I just pat them as I walk by. My portrait of Jimmy is different. His son gave me the portrait of his dad. It was taken shortly before Jimmy's untimely death. Jimmy just sits there in the room where I work and when I walk by he offers me counseling. He always called me Mr. Biggs, just couldn't say Briggs. More often than not he will tell me not to do something or I shouldn't have done something. Occasionally he will give me a big smile and say – way to go: I like that. In life Jimmy was held in high esteem for his skill with the tractor he used for cutting the grass for Georgia College. It was said that he could make that tractor go into impossible places. After Jimmy died, I asked Georgia College to honor Jimmy for his dedication to his work and so they did. Georgia College placed a bronze plaque in a building on their campus, near where Jimmy worked. Not a bad honor when you consider that Jimmy was illiterate.

Many people do not believe in a spirit world but I do. And for that reason I believe Jimmy and I can talk now due to our strong bond of friendship that developed over the years that Jimmy worked for me. As an example of that friendship one night Jimmy couldn't sleep and so he called his "Auntie." His Aunt Thelma Blassingame was more like a mother to Jimmy. He dearly loved her and she returned that love, so when Jimmy was troubled he would call her. This night Jimmy was worried about me. He called his aunt and told her "he was worried about Mr. Biggs." Thelma told Jimmy to go out to my house and check otherwise he wouldn't get any rest and that is what he did. Jimmy drove out to my house in the middle of the night, made sure everything was alright and then went back home.

Jimmy is not as involved with me as my favorite two clowns. Jimmy just tries to keep me out of trouble by giving me his advice. One of those two clowns continually tries to meddle in my business but the other clown is quick to point out everything will be okay and not to worry. If you could see their faces you would understand them a little better.

The shorter of the two is Mr. Wise Guy. One look at his face and you can tell by the smirk that he thinks he as all of the answers. And he is quick to give you his opinion. Mr. Simpatico is a little taller than his buddy and heavier. His face is always warm and friendly and ready to offer you a kind word. You can never be down with a friend like Simpatico to lift you up.

Every night, before I go to sleep, Mr. Wise Guy and Mr. Simpatico and I have a brief talk. Then I say my prayers and then it is off to sleep I go. The next morning the two of them are waiting for me and it begins all over again. If it wasn't for Mr. Simpatico to give me balance, Mr. Wise Guy would keep me ticked off all the time.

The following selection is taken from The Floridians, *an historical novel about two generations of a family who moved to Florida during its territorial days. The two characters in this scene are Ellen, whose husband, Joseph White, has become prominent in diplomatic circles of Europe, as well as Florida, and their friend, Richard Wilde, a widower who is also Joseph's business partner. The two families are in Florence, Italy, combining pleasure with business.*

THE FLORIDIANS
BY
MARGARET ANDERSON UHLER

Chapter Twelve

CHAPTER TWELVE:
RICHARD
1833

The Wilde family arrived in due course, the boys ready to take Florence by storm. Kate and Ellen made certain their education was not neglected, and they proved to be, for the most part, avid students. In no time they had mastered the rudiments of Italian phrases and pronunciation. While they were sometimes less than enthusiastic about the museums and churches that were forced on them, the boys were fascinated with the Ponte Vecchio and its myriad little shops lining each side.

"Boys," Ellen said at the end of a morning's assault on the Uffizi Gallery, "you've been such good, sober students that I think you've earned a reward. How about a hearty meal in a trattoria, where the waiters are loud and jolly."

All in all, Ellen and Joseph looked forward to many months of good times in the company of their favorite people.

One of the Whites' new acquaintances was an old friend of Richard's, the brilliant sculptor Horatio Greenough, who had been in Florence for several months. He had been commissioned to sculpt a statue of George Washington for the national capitol. He was in his element having such a prestigious assignment, besides being so close to as much Carrara marble as he could ever want.

Richard, Horatio, Joseph and Ellen were on the terrace of the Whites' villa on a balmy spring day that brought to mind the landscapes of Renaissance paintings. From the hillside they looked down at the sparkling Arno, out over red tiled roofs, and the lofty profile of the Duomo silhouetted against the sky.

Richard and Horatio had agreed to leave their respective works long enough to indulge in a relaxing lunch with the Whites. The heady scent of orange blossoms combined with the taste of mouth-watering calzones, cooked by the ebullient Graciella and served with Vino Corso Blanco, had them all a little giddy. Dessert was *tirumisu*, a cake and custard concoction that made them think of trifle, except that it was flavored with amaretto. Horatio had a particular fondness for it.

"Ellen, do you think you could persuade Graciella to part with another serving of that incomparable kissa-me-foo? It's something to faint over. There's a good girl."

He had recently sent a drawing of his proposed statue to a friend, whose response to it puzzled him.

"I heard from Edward Everett yesterday, and he didn't like my drawing. I can't believe him! He doesn't like *the placement of the right hand*! Even worse, he objects to the nudity! Can you believe that?"

Richard stared in disbelief. "Horatio! I didn't hear what I thought I heard, did I? You're not plotting a *nekkid* George Washington! My God, man, you've been in Italy too long. You've gone all Michelangelo on us! The United States Capitol's not the Sistine Chapel, for God's sake. Don't you know Americans will never stand for a nekkid statue in their capitol?"

"Not *nekkid*, Richard. *Nude*."

"Same thing."

"Is not. *Na-ked* is obscenity. *Nekkid's* worse. *Nude* is art."

Joseph joined the debate. "Is that so? Well, just try telling that to Andy Jackson's frontiersmen. They're all over the capitol these days, you know. The Houdon sculpture you're using as a model for the head is fine, but do you have any idea what Washington's rump looked like? It was nothing like that Timothy tight-ass Zeus you're using as a model for the rest of him. In fact, according to my father, from behind he looked like the back end of a stagecoach with both doors open."

"Are you suggesting," said Horatio, "that if someone told him to haul ass, he'd have had to make two trips?"

"At least. It's a dangerous thing, Horatio, to address a work of art to a degree of refinement that does not exist among those who'll see it. Trust me on this. Your friend, Everett, knows what he's talking about."

Ellen agreed. "Americans aren't as comfortable with nudity as Europeans are, and they would think a na-ked (or nekkid either) George Washington a sacrilege. You really better come up with something else."

"Oh, all right, all right. In that case, I'll have to divert myself with other commissions. Joe, that noble but balding brow of yours cries out to be immortalized in marble. And the charming Elena bellissima will make a perfect companion. After all, what's the point of groveling around wealthy friends if not to let them keep me in commissions? Come on, you two. Console me for a properly clad but dull Washington by letting me create two stunning busts. Ellen, your beauty's at its peak now; in a few years you'll be alas, fat and wrinkled. And, Joe, you need to be sculpted before you get any older or your brow reaches all the way to the back of your neck.'"

"Do I get to wear my toga?" Joseph asked. "I don't fancy myself marbleized in casual attire. And, Ellen, you must be sure to wear the fetching black gown and face-covering veil you wore for your audience with the Pope."

"You can both be stitch-starch nekkid for all I care—I'm still only doing your heads."

Horatio finished the last crumb of tiramisu and pressed the napkin to his lips.

****

It was a unique experience for the Whites, but they did, indeed, commission Horatio to carve their busts. Horatio's studio was a fascinating place with his works in progress staring from their niches. His face took on an exalted expression as he stroked his marble the way a lover strokes living flesh.

"I found my visits to the quarries among the most exhilarating experiences of my life. I actually felt connected to the great Renaissance sculptors, standing where they stood, gazing on the same scene."

His young assistant, Paolo, wearing the traditional paper hat to keep the marble dust out of his hair, bustled about, sweeping up the shavings that coated the floor and himself with a fine, powdery dust. It was hard to sit still for so long at a time, and Ellen kept wanting to chat. Horatio, though, who was full of banter at other times, was so absorbed in his work that he wouldn't amuse her at all. Marble dust clung to everything, skin, clothes, hair—and especially her nose. If she wasn't scratching, she was sneezing.

The day finally came that Horatio finished Ellen's bust and started on Joseph's. Joseph was more stoical than she, and his was finished in a good bit less time. Horatio and Richard brought the busts to the Whites' villa for the unveiling.

Horatio removed the covers and all were struck speechless. The strength in Joseph's noble face almost breathed in its marble likeness. And Ellen was so taken with hers that, like Narcissus, she was in grave danger of admiring herself to death.

"These will grace the drawing room at Casa Bianca, Horatio, and we'll never see them without remembering this happy time."

****

To the great relief of the friends, Horatio abandoned the idea of a nude Washington. Instead, the subject was seated, with one arm raised in the attitude of a Roman emperor, bare only from the waist up and draped below the waist.

"My fee for this ten and a half-foot high, twenty-ton statue is $5,000," he said. "But the cost of shipping and then placing it in the rotunda of the capitol will probably come to $20,000 or more. I fear most Americans will be scandalized."

Well, maybe not as scandalized as they would have been with a nude Washington, Ellen thought.

During the winter Ellen was ill again, and the doctor felt that she should not accompany Joseph to Paris. Joseph was particularly grateful, therefore, for the presence of the Wildes, who he knew would look after her in his absence. "It's going to be hard to tear myself away from here," Joseph said as he and Ellen breakfasted on the patio and looked down on the houses below with their tile roofs and flower-crammed yards. "But I need to get to Paris to work on the Murat case, as well as the other ones I have there. Even with all there is against a successful conclusion, I'll do what I can to earn the confidence this strange young man has placed in me."

After he had been gone for about a month, a letter came bearing unwelcome but not surprising news about the Murat case:

> *Even the combined influences of the Secretary of State and the United States Minister to France couldn't prevail against French political intrigue. Achille had hoped that my cordial relations with the Emperor Louis Philippe would be of some benefit, in view of the emperor's personal dislike of Achille. But the emperor suspected that Achille had ambitions to usurp his throne. My failure to win the case was a disappointment to me, though not an unexpected one. To Achille it was a crushing blow and his precarious general condition is not relieved.*

****

While Joseph was away, Richard and Kate were solicitous for Ellen's welfare, but Richard was increasingly absorbed in his Dante research. His enthusiasm was so contagious that even Ellen began to get caught up in it and eased up from her previous resistance to Catholic literature. After a late lunch at Richard's house, they strolled behind the rest of the party, Kate, Horatio, and two other guests, and the intensity of their discussion isolated them more and more. A stone bench in the shade of an umbrella pine offered itself as an inviting spot to sit and talk-or maybe argue.

"You see, Richard, Dante was never a part of my Presbyterian upbringing. We were more familiar with Milton's grand concepts of heaven and hell."

"Ah, but now that you're in Dante's home town," he answered, "you have a golden opportunity to overcome your early deprivation—not to mention your *incomprehensible* aversion to Catholicism."

She protested. "Richard, as an intelligent, educated man, how can you go along with the ignorant, superstitious practices of the Catholic Church? And Dante is its leading spokesman. How can any thinking person not question, for instance, the blind acceptance of miracles that are nothing more than natural occurrences?"

"My dear unbelieving Ellen, if you ramble around Italy long enough, you likely will stumble across at least one small miracle. Of course, it won't be a Protestant one, there being no such thing in Italy."

Richard's smirk was intended to vex. He paused so that he faced her. By now, he had sparked her spirit of debate. She sat down on the bench and invited him to sit beside her. She smiled smugly and spoke.

"No Protestant miracles? Well. Tell me, my good man, what did *the Pope* say to *you* when you had *your private* audience with him?"

"Touché! Touché!" Richard leaned forward and smiled, even as he conceded her point. "So you did indeed manage one rather impressive miracle of the Presbyterian persuasion. It's no match I am for such a barbed wit, and I stand humbled in your exalted presence."

Then he turned guileless blue eyes at her and added with mock solemnity, "All he said to me was, 'My son, Where the hell did you get that god-awful cravat?'"

"Richard," Ellen exploded, "you're downright sacrilegious! I have more respect for the Pope than you do." Then she couldn't resist adding, "Know him better, too."

They both laughed. The two enjoyed their religious sparring. He had an unfailing knack for deflating what he called her "pompous puritanism." His approach to religion was more lighthearted than Ellen's. Finally, at his urging, she agreed to read Dante's unforgettable pilgrimage to salvation and found herself swept up in the splendor of the poetry and the soaring intellect that created it. But the more deeply she became immersed in its epic majesty, the more questions she had.

****

One sunny morning after Joseph's return from Paris, Ellen answered a knock at the door to find Richard with some papers in his hand.

"Top o' the mornin' to you, lass. Where's Himself?"

"Good morning, Richard. Himself had some early morning business to tend to in town. He should be home before lunchtime, though. Why don't you stay and eat with us?"

"Thanks, I'd love to. And it's no matter that Joe's not here. I need his advice on some legal affairs before he sets off for Madrid, but you and I still have much to discuss about my friend Dante while we await your husband's return."

"Let's sit in the morning room and see if we can sort out some ideas. I'll ring for tea. Joseph's going back to Madrid in about a week."

The room was bright with the morning sun streaming through the windows. Richard leaned against the marble fireplace and traced the slender veins with his finger.

"Where were we when we last talked?"

"You see, Richard, I have trouble reconciling Dante's obvious genius with the superstition—it always comes back to that—that permeates the Catholic Church. Ignorance and superstition are soul mates, and I see them all around me here in Italy."

"Well, maybe superstition is in the eye of the beholder. What, specifically, do you have in mind?" Richard stood before her, eyes alert.

"The first thing is the nearly toeless right foot on the statue of Saint Peter in the cathedral in Rome. How can you justify centuries of people kissing away *the toes of a bronze statue*, no less? That sounds like idolatry to me. And, yet, Dante, the genius, is the spokesman for the church that fosters it."

Richard placed his cup on the nearby table and paced the room.

"The thing is Dante probably saw sin in its larger context. I doubt that he ever gave much thought to Saint Peter's worn toes. It's been my observation that Italians are enthusiastic kissers, anyway. You've seen that shiny right breast on the lovely little statue of Juliet in Verona, haven't you? And you do know why it looks so bright while the rest of the statue looks dull with age, don't you?"

"I guess you'd say it's centuries of being kissed by these ardent Italians is why."

"Of course. I think they must have a motto: if you want it to shine, kiss it. Don't much matter whether it's a toe or a breast." He watched Ellen closely, expecting a smile. But she was only getting started so she let that remark go.

"And then, there's his hatred—yes *hatred*—of any faith except his own. He has no religious tolerance at all."

Richard's voice became soft. "Quite true, my beautiful heretic. But he was a medieval Catholic. We are all children of our own time, and he was a child of the age that saw heresy as a mortal sin and also as a crime against the state. Have you never heard the adage, `Time makes ancient good uncouth'? We gasp in horror at the vision of Mohammed, for instance, in a circle of hell. To Dante, he was not a religious leader, but an anti-Christian who richly deserved to suffer eternal torments.

We've come a long way toward tolerance in four hundred years. In another four hundred years, our descendants may find certain of our attitudes equally barbaric."

Ellen turned away. "And I don't understand Purgatory at all. If there were such a place, the Bible would surely mention it. Since it doesn't, I simply can't believe in it."

She looked back at Richard and moved over to the fireplace. She felt warm, and as usual, at a disadvantage when Richard hovered about her. He came and stood at her side, still in a reconciling posture.

"Oh, never you mind about that, lass. Purgatory's a state of the soul, like heaven and hell, not a geographical location. When you get there, you'll know right where you are, whether you believe in it or no." He sounded annoyingly cocky.

"You're still incorrigible, Richard, but I'm not done yet," she flung back at him. "I want to know about the poor heretic, Manfred, who can't even break *into* Purgatory. Other heretics, like Mohammed, are in hell, but since he's not there, why isn't he impatient to get into heaven rather than into Purgatory?"

"Manfred, you see," explained Richard, "in his stubbornness, was disobedient to the Church. Though his deathbed repentance keeps him from the fires of hell, he did keep God waiting. Now he has to wait for thirty times the period of his disobedience. Even so, the fact that he's there ensures his eventual acceptance into heaven. He could still be waiting at the base of that cliff clamoring to begin his ascent through Purgatory, *when you get there*." He laughed lightly.

"I doubt that! I was brought up on hellfire, so I can relate to the *Inferno*. Purgatory, though, I cannot accept. Manfred's final repentance should have him safely installed in heaven, not dragging around for centuries waiting for someone else's prayers to shorten his suffering."

"Very well, let's sit down in peace. If we can't agree on Purgatory, let's entertain ourselves by trying to relate the entire *Commedia* to our own lives."

They made themselves comfortable and Richard continued. "Dante himself said, `Its subject is Man, in so far as by merit or demerit in the exercise of free will he is exposed to the rewards or punishments of justice.' Dante does not allow us to be slaves of accident or environment. To appreciate him fully, we must believe in our free will, and the choices we make decide our eternity."

"Well, so far, I don't quarrel with him. That sounds pretty Presbyterian to me."

By now Richard and Ellen were in some accord.

"Dante, like all great writers, knew that human nature doesn't change, regardless of external factors. Whatever is medieval and Catholic, for instance, may not be valid forever, but that which is ethical and human is everlasting. With our nineteenth century concepts of sin, you and I would arrange hell quite differently if we were designing it for our own age, now, wouldn't we?" His expression became pensive.

"I see what you mean, Richard. It wouldn't occur to me, to think of heresy as any sin at all, only a difference of opinion. I don't much think I'd condemn gluttons, either."

"Exactly," Richard added and then was off again. "And how about the usurers? In Dante's time, usury meant charging any interest for money. The Church was adamant about that. But Dante's usurers are our bankers, and where would we be without them? Notice, too, how the punishment fits the sin."

His voice softened. "As the carnal lovers, Francesca and Paolo, surrendered to the storm of their passions, they must now spend eternity being blown about unceasingly and being buffeted by the `black whirlwind,' having neither pleasure in nor escape from each other. What had seemed so bright and beautiful is now revealed in all its stark ugliness: the forbidden, perverted, twisted love, the breaking of marriage vows. . ." He broke off abruptly, leaving his final words suspended in the air.

All of a sudden, Richard appeared agitated and nervous. He turned and strode to the door as if he were in a hurry to leave.

"Richard," Ellen said in surprise, "surely you aren't leaving just now? Why are you in such a hurry? Did I score more points than you allow?"

Her question was ventured lightly, but clearly something had disturbed him.

"I have to get back to work. Our discussion has. . .I've stayed away too long." His words were curt, and he left without a sip of his fresh tea and without waiting for Joseph.

What, Ellen wondered, *has happened?* She closed her eyes for a second, seeing Richard's distressed face. *What could have prompted such an abrupt departure?*

ALGONQUIAN
Irwin Gates

My name is Algonquian. I am standing before this revival meeting to confess my out-of-control behavior. My eating is completely off the chart. In my youth I was very thin, but as I grew I got so wide that people joked I was as wide as the space between the Rocky and Allegheny Mountains. When I heard what was being said, I dropped 65 pounds to show that I can reduce. However, like many others, I picked up even more weight. When word got out that I had gained more weight, it made me so angry that I actually changed color. In my fury, I started tearing things apart and separating people from each other as they took sides. I thought I was gone for sure.

I got help and slowly got myself back into control. When I was normal, people loved me and forgave my out-of-control behavior. I attribute their forgiveness to the grace of God. People were kind, even moving next door. They helped me with construction, putting up trusses, building retaining walls, and even installing locks for my new home. They even built a lake for fishing, recreation, water transportation and personal use. Even so, all was not peaches and cream. I have trouble with changing my mind. I start out in one direction and end up going another. To tell the truth, I meander around and seem to get nowhere. In my wanderings, I visited ten states, but because of my forgiven state I helped people with their surveying. I laid out lakes, dams, locks, storage reservoirs, and levees, and brought people together from different areas of the country. I have united people from Minnesota to Louisiana. Through God's grace, I have done some good. Newcomers call me Mississippi.

Busy Boxer
Doyle Boyd

She sprang from her corner
And came out fighting
To teach a group of retirees
The fine art of writing

The Ole Red Rooster
Martha Chandler Tomlin

"Martha, go to the store for me. Tell Jim to send me five pounds of sugar," Mother said to me, her young and defenseless child.

"Mother, I don't want to go. That bad rooster is in the backyard. I'm really scared of him."

"Go on, Martha. The rooster won't hurt you. If you're scared of him, get one of Jim's walking sticks to take with you." From the umbrella stand in the hall, I chose the biggest walking cane in my daddy's collection.

Hesitating on the back steps, I surveyed the backyard looking for the red rooster. I was watching for him while he was watching for me. I thought that if I tip-toed past the henhouse, I could make a run for the gate and safety.

The rooster had different ideas. He was lurking behind the henhouse observing and thinking "Here comes that little girl. She's afraid of me; I think I'll scare her. I'm ready to fight."

Just as I thought I had made it safely to the gate, the rooster rushed from his hiding place behind the henhouse. He was in attack mode, wings lowered to sweep the ground and a determined and evil glint in his beady eyes. As he came toward me, I realized I was in grave danger. Without taking aim, I gave a mighty swing with Daddy's cane. The rooster silently fell to the ground and lay there motionless.

My mother had been watching me from her bedroom window; she screamed to Daisy, our help, "Martha's killed my rooster!" Both rushed to the yard. The three of us stood watching this slain mighty ruler of our chicken house. I was silent. Mother told me, "Martha, go on to the store and get my sugar." I gladly left the scene of my crime.

When I returned with the sugar, Mother and Daisy stood watching a dazed rooster moving very slowly. He appeared not to know what had hit him.

"What happened?" I asked.

"Daisy poured water on his head and he came to," Mother stated in a hushed tone.

I stood looking at this subdued bird until I was told to take the sugar to the kitchen. I went. I was feeling very sad and wanted to cry; Mother and Daisy loved that horrible rooster more than me.

The Binnickers:
South Carolina Swamp Women
Mary B. Purcell

There were seven of them in the beginning, but they killed off four. I knew them. They were not strangers to adversity, disease, and death. The three girls who survived were tough, lean, and hungry. Beauty hid between smudges of dirt on suntanned skin. In cotton dresses full of holes, they worked and played, disregarding the snakes and 'gators but paying close attention to the lessons of life taught by Black Ankle Swamp.

They grew up catching fish and butchering hogs. And they were good at both. One of the girls toted a gun . . . all three carried knives. They planted, plowed, and made compost from the leavings—learning early how to make something from nothing.

When South Carolina decided to chase the tourists' dollars, the state brought in big CATs to push up the trees, leaving the swamp and the girls high and dry. Unable to eke out a living, the girls and their families migrated to the big city of Savannah, Georgia.

I ran into one of them the other day. She was sitting in an upscale Boston restaurant, looking very attorney-like in her expensive blue suit and white silk blouse; hair perfectly coiffed; her fingers dancing on the keyboard of her laptop computer, which was balanced precisely at the edge of the table where the white starched cloth folded over the edge. As I approached, she pointed to the chair opposite her. Immediately, a waiter appeared.

"We'll have two sweet iced teas," she said.

"Perhaps madam would like to see our award winning wine list. We don't serve iced tea." He smiled that artificial smile that waiters use when they are annoyed with a customer.

The laptop snapped shut. She turned her Binnicker blues so that she was staring directly into his Boston browns. "I am not interested in your wines, sir. My sister and I are from the South, and we'll have two sweet iced teas."

I watched as the words the waiter wished to say beat against the sides of his cheeks and rolled around inside his mouth. He straightened his frame, "Yes, madam," he said, as he slowly turned and disappeared.

I didn't argue with her either. He had only looked into her Binnicker blues. I, on the other hand, had seen her butcher a hog.

A Significant Event
A Woman's Heart Attack*
Susan Lindsley

*Previously published: Kevin Coyle and Aimee Caruso, editors:
The Petigru Review, Vol. I, The South Carolina Writers Workshop, pp. 112-117, 2007.

Who wants to be found dead on the toilet while the cat rubs figure eights around your legs to get you to pet her?

Your bowels wake you, and you lie still, keep your eyes closed and listen to your partner's steady breathing. You try to move slowly so you don't wake her, but your gut warns you to hurry. You slip out from under the covers, and as your feet hit the floor, the coldness runs up your legs and chases shivers along your back. Cold is good for sleeping, but not for walking around in the dark. You close the door to the bathroom and flick on the light; before you reach the john, the cat trots in to welcome you to morning, not realizing it is only 4:00 a.m.

You hurry to the john, and as you sit, your bowels cramp and nausea begins to niggle at you. Too much restaurant supper last night. More than a touch of indigestion? You look at the trash can, its liner almost full. Well, at least if you do vomit you can jerk out the liner and use the metal can. It'll wash. You think back to the time you had salmonella and vomited while diarrhea racked your guts. The thought brings a shiver as sweat begins to wet your clothes. The nausea seems to move upward a bit and then turn to pain. Sharp pain.

And the cat twines around your ankles, her tail like a noodle whip as she mews to ask for petting. The spasms end and the nausea passes. But the sharp aching continues just beneath your left breast, and the sweat is unbelievable. When was the last time you had a hot flash? It's been several years, but none like this, with sweat trickling down. Weakness creeps over you. As you wash your hands, you look at yourself in the mirror and think, I must be sick. I'm pale as the walls.

And your eyes have sunk into purple pools.

Although the nausea has passed, the pre-nausea sweat you always had just before you emptied your stomach has not only continued but seems to be intensifying. You rest your hands on the edge of the basin and lean over, remembering your mother.

She had indigestion. She thought. You weren't there, but you remember the story your Aunt Katie told later. In Hawaii, they traveled by boat from one island to another, and on the way your mama got to feeling bad. Upset stomach, she told Katie. Maybe a touch of seasickness.

When they arrived at their hotel, instead of going to supper with the group, she told Katie she would lie down until her indigestion passed.

About 90 minutes later, when Katie returned to their room from supper, she found your mama dead of a heart attack.

Are you having a heart attack? No pain down the left arm. No pain up the neck. No feeling of pressure.

You are two years older than your mama when she died. And older than the grandmother you never knew who also thought she had indigestion and died of a heart attack in the five minutes her daughter (your mama) was gone to the kitchen for a bi-carb to relieve the gas pressure.

You reach for the aspirin. You quit taking it two months ago when you had surgery, so you blame yourself if it is a heart attack. You pop one pill, grab the glass, get enough water to wash down the ASA, put the cat out into the den, and head back to the bedroom.

"Sweetheart," you call her. She answers with a sleep-filled murmur.

"Please wake up. I think I'm sick." You don't want to tell her you're having a heart attack. Let her wake up good before you scare the very daylights out of her.

She sits up. "What's the matter?"

You reach for your slacks and as you slip them on you answer. "I've got some funny feelings in my chest. I think I'm having a heart attack."

She jumps up and hurries into her clothes, dressed long before you tie your shoes.

You grab your sweatshirt. It's cold out, below freezing. Near 60 inside, but still you sweat while shivering.

You head downstairs together and your three animals begin to dance around you, happy to see the day start early. The stairs seem to go on forever as your legs wobble from weakness. You grip the single banister with both hands, and once on the first floor you sit in the lounge chair by the front door while she dashes to the phone to call 911. Her voice reaches you from the kitchen as she gives information, and before she returns to you, she puts the animals out—the cats into the guest bedroom and the dog into the basement so they can't escape when the EMTs arrive.

Red lights flash through the glass panels in the front door. Your partner opens it for two uniformed EMTs to enter, one a tall lanky man and the other a younger woman, both carrying an emergency kit. They announce that they are the "first responders" and that the ambulance crew will be along.

The woman kneels at your feet and begins to ask questions. As you talk with her, you become aware than the pain has gone, the sweating has lessened, but you are still shivering with cold. Has the aspirin done its job and stopped the heart attack—if it were a heart attack?

Her hands are strong and deft as she checks pulse, blood pressure and temperature, but her voice is light, as if she's having an afternoon tea rather than on a life-saving mission. You realize she is trying to help you relax and not worry about what is happening.

The two ambulance EMTs arrive with a stretcher. You won't remember much about being put on the stretcher, but you'll never forget the trip to their vehicle. The city tore up the sidewalk two weeks ago and has not yet re-paved it. The six-inch deep hole extends from one end of the yard to the other; boards line the opening, and red flagging is pulled taut alongside. The EMTs lift the stretcher, kick down the red flagging, and transport you across the ditch. You hear their feet squish in the mud.

In you go, head first, and the two medics confer and then begin the journey to Emory Hospital. One straps a tourniquet around your left arm, and you say, "I'm left-handed. Please don't start an IV there."

"We have to," he says. "It's standard procedure."

Your right arm is against the wall. You decide it's too much effort to argue and he sticks the IV needle into the elbow joint. You won't be bending the arm or using it for much with the needle there. But he does not start Ringers or any other fluids.

"What're you doing?" He calls to the driver when the ambulance pulls into a bank parking lot.

"Turning around. I took a wrong turn."

Glad you weren't dying.

You finally arrive at the Emory Emergency room, and your partner appears from nowhere. How did she get here so fast? She had to feed the animals after she released them from their short-term lock-ups.

Voices direct the EMTs to a cubicle as nurses and a doctor enter behind you. One slaps a nitroglycerine patch on your chest. Another brings in an IV pole. Now you decide is time to argue about the location of that needle, and the nurse inserts a new one in the other arm, above the hand, so you can use that arm also. The elbow needle gets pulled out.

All the chest pain is gone. You feel good. And hungry. You ask for food, but are told no, you're going to have a cath, so you have to wait.

The doctor asks if you had pain in your arm or in your neck.

You answer no and ask the doctor if you had a heart attack.

"I'd say you have an insignificant cardiac event," he replies.

Your partner came prepared, for here comes the ER clerk for insurance information and your partner pulls out your Blue Cross card.

You wait. And wait, from 5 a.m. until close to 1 p.m. before a cath lab is free. All you will remember about that procedure is saying to the doctor, "That hurts," and they give you enough meds to knock you out.

Three stents and an hour later, you're back in your room, your right leg strapped so you can't move it and open up your artery. When the doctor stops by, he changes his diagnosis to "significant cardiac event."

Home again Monday afternoon, and Tuesday morning, you receive a telephone call that the Old Capital Press wants to publish your book.

Even better, you weren't found dead on the toilet.

Friends
Patricia S. Byrd

The sky is grey—

I like it that way.

The clouds are my friends

That my Maker sends

To hover over His child

And enfold me for a while.

The Wings of Icarus
Barry Darugar

"My son the doctor," my father announced, "He will sew you up." He pointed to me as his surprised and bewildered patient's hazel eyes opened wide.

"Don't you worry, I'm right here with him," he reassured his patient. Learning through apprenticeship had been an old tradition in Iran, but I was merely a sophomore in pre-med; I hadn't even begun my hospital rotations. Fortunately, I was already familiar with the instruments and sutures. He had shown me how to place sutures and repair lacerations. I can still remember what he told me, step by step:

> *Start at one end of the laceration, one fifth of an inch from the edge of it on the right. The needle you hold in your right hand goes in through the skin while the tweezers in your left hand hold the skin steady. Push the needle through the thickness of the cut to the other side of skin, and push it out one-fifth of an inch from the edge and tie the suture in a knot. Then turn the needle around and repeat the process and continue toward the end of the laceration. The suture line will look like a nice zipper sewn over the edges of the laceration.*

He showed me how to place individual sutures and emphasized the importance of tying square knots. I learned the difference between absorbable cat gut and less irritating dexon. He told me silk and nylon will always remain in the body because they are nonabsorbable.

"You can't use silk inside the wound," he said, and asked me to change to catgut. On another occasion, I alarmed him when I started to numb the skin too close to an abscessed cyst. "Stop! Don't inject so close to the infected site or you will spread the germs," he shouted. "Freeze it with ethyl chloride." He showed me how to spray with the left hand until the snow-white dust appeared on the surface of the abscess and then push the hook-shaped knife in, slicing forward and up for an inch to let the puss out. He guided my hands through that procedure. A few days later, the grateful and healed patient came in ready to kiss my hand as if I were a deity.

As I advanced through pre-med and medical school I became more self-confident and began to see my father as a less than perfect man. At times I even perceived him as clumsy. To show off, I closed a patient's wound with a new technical procedure, hiding the sutures inside the wound, making it look like the cut was glued together. I used

Betadine, a painless disinfectant, instead of pain producing iodine. I argued about using newer tests and medications.

One day during my rebellious and insolent period, my father showed me a feverish patient with a temperature of 103.The patient was pale and weak with nausea, vomiting, and stomach pain. She had a rash all over her body. I immediately jumped in with a diagnosis of ricketsial disease, a disease equivalent to Rocky Mountain Spotted Fever. My father told me, "Smell the patient."

"He smells sick."

"No, it's the distinct odor of typhoid," he said.

"You can't be serious! You ought to run the serum test or a blood culture to be sure."

"My indigent patients can't afford the high price of lab tests. I diagnose with my hands, nose, and eyes," my father answered.

"Yes, but you practice stone age medicine." I huffed and walked out in protest. I remained hostile until three months later when our infectious disease professor mentioned that typhoid patients have a distinct odor caused by the typhoid bacilli.

However, my boorish behavior continued a while longer. Our family was in the process of buying a car. My parents and I looked at several models, but my father rejected them all. He labeled the Cadillac as a gas guzzler, the Mercedes too expensive, the Peugeot too shoddy, and the Fiat as standing for "Failure in Automotive Technology." He eventually settled on a cream color 54 Chevrolet Bel Air.

I quickly learned how to drive and passed the driving test, but my father had a hard time coordinating the clutch and the gas, as well as changing gears and steering at the same time. I berated him when he ran the car into our garage wall one day and into a ditch the next day. I clicked my tongue in disgust and said, "It's not that difficult to drive a car." My father ignored my comments, which fueled my anger even more. "Even young kids can drive a car, I can't figure out why you can't." I stomped my feet and walked off.

I was too young and also stressed by the demands of medical school on my mind and body. Furthermore, I was going through a late teenage surge of testosterone-related aggressiveness.

At the same time that I was going through my emotional upheaval, my father was also changing. He'd lost some weight, and then gained it all back and plus more. He craved candy bars and ice cream, and often misread road signs. I suspected he was a diabetic, but what I didn't know then was that he already knew about his illness and concealed it from the rest of us. The changes in my father were upsetting my mother.

****

My own behavior worried and upset my mother even more than my father's declining health. She noticed the signs of sexual awakening in me. The young girl who had worked for us for five years ever since she was twelve, began to appear differently to me. I'd never paid much attention before, but her developing breasts and buttocks combined with my raging hormones caused me to take notice and make sexual advances toward her. Initially harmless, my overtures later became emboldened by her minimal protests and even hints of encouragement. I eventually had sex with her, although fearing pregnancy, she would not allow vaginal intercourse. My mother came home unexpectedly one day and discovered me amidst orgasmic thrusts against the nude pear-shaped ass of our young maid. My mother's eyes sparked with surprise and anger. She threw our maid's clothes at her and ordered her to go to her room and wait. My mother walked toward me and slapped my face twice as hard as she could. I was already paralyzed by fear and now stood there stunned and speechless. "Your father will deal with you later." She stomped out of the room.

That night, I heard my parents argue. I imagine my father like most other Persian fathers made light of the incident by saying, "Boys will be boys." I can imagine my father concealing his smile. *That's my boy. It's about time. I was beginning to wonder about him.*

The next morning, my mother lectured me on the teachings of the Prophet Baha-u-llah and the great rewards of living a pious life. She indicated that my soul was facing the imminent danger of eternal doom for corrupting an innocent young girl. I felt thoroughly guilty and ashamed and asked repeatedly for my mom's forgiveness, which she gave me. But my mother was a practical woman; she removed any possible temptation by replacing the young maid with an old woman.

****

When I returned home, after completing medical school, my father could barely see. He often lost his way when returning home. My mother forbade him from going out by himself, especially to prevent him from eating sweets that aggravated his diabetic condition. My father, like a naughty boy, sneaked out anyway and bought ice cream and candy bars, and would come home having peed in his pants and feeling depressed.

My father's forays into the streets and his soiling his pants with a mix of urine and feces eventually led to an abscess on his left buttock near the base of his spine.

"Let me lance it for you," I asked him.

"I won't let a wet behind the ears boy touch me," he growled.

I realized he was paying me back for my insolences of the past. My mother had to beg him to let me drain the abscess. He consented only after my mother assured him I was a fully accredited doctor and licensed to perform surgery.

Yet he screamed. "Take it easy dammit," he scolded me.

When I incised the abscess and puss flowed out and over the sheets, he almost jumped off the bed.

"You're killing me," he shouted, "Didn't I teach you how to use Novocain?"

He lay there prone on the table, his bare bottom exposed like a child who is surrendering to punishment. He was at my mercy. I recalled as a child wanting to kill him when I saw him kissing a young widow in his clinic, but at that time he was a towering figure and I was just a small boy.

" No Dad, I'm not trying to kill you," I answered, "But this is an abscess, and you yourself told me not to inject Novocain in and around an abscess."

My perception of his behavior toward young women changed later as I entered the practice of the healing arts myself. I recognized his acts for what they really were. He was the benevolent father to the widows and to children who sorely missed their own fathers.

Even though my father healed, his mind deteriorated even more, and since my mother was at her wits' end, I sent her off to the Caspian seashore to visit my sister for a few days of rest. I didn't know then that this was my last chance to take care of my father. I lifted his frail body into the bath tub every day and washed his arms, legs and torso. I wiped the dirt off his feet and cleaned the caked feces off his buttocks. His eyes were trusting, and in the warm bath tub he calmed and relaxed and let me clean and wash him.

I recalled when I was a young kid in the *hammom*, the public bath, and my father washed my back with soap and *Keeseh*, peeling a week's dirt off my body. He showed me how to use pumice on the soles my feet.

"Dad, do you remember sewing my chin when I fell off the cherry tree in the back yard? Or was it the pomegranate tree I fell from when I was five years old?" I asked.

"You were only four, but you were such a brave boy," he answered.

"I think I was in shock, in a daze," I said.

He smiled. "But you specifically asked for me and wouldn't let anyone else fix you." My father looked proud - the old glitter back in his eyes.

"I trusted only you, Dad." I toweled his body as I drained the bath tub. "I trust you now."

My father smiled. "Why do you think I let you treat me?"

This was the most lucid my father was during that week, our last day alone together.

"Son, I am ready to die." He looked into my eyes. "Why don't you inject me with a large dose of insulin," he begged.

"No, Dad. You'll be all right again." I held my breath; I felt tightness in the back of my neck.

A month later, at sunset, my mother had to pull their car onto the shoulder of the highway between Karaj and Teheran. My father was making gurgling noises and was clasping at his chest. My mother told me after his death that she held on to him on the front seat and whispered sweetly in his ears, like a mother to a hurt child, as my father clutched at his heart. She wiped perspiration from his forehead and let him rest his head between her bosoms. I can envision my mother watching that particular sunset. I can imagine the goddess of the sun gathering her brood and nestling behind the mountains, and I can see Tehran's saffron clouds close across the blue sky like a giant curtain.

꿍ꞇꙅ

Soft summer breezes

Like the breath of an angel,

Brush against my cheek.

-M.T. Knight

Play Ball!
Ed Bzdyk

This should be a funny story about a young boy who seriously thought he could play ball.

Actually, he didn't realize that he could not. It was not a question of just not wanting to put in the effort. It was not that he had any physical impediments. In fact, he was just about as healthy of mind and body as any other spirited young fellow in the early 1950s.

He did quite well scholastically without having to expend too much energy. While he never set about to practice hitting the ball, he figured that when "he was ready," he would just turn to and get started. As self-assured as he was that this was possible, he decided that the first and most important step in the process would be to have a picture taken of himself, posing with a bat. This, he concluded, would provide him sufficient impetus to continue with the process of becoming proficient in hitting a ball with the bat. After all, all he would have to do was look at the picture and imagine how well he would be able to perform as a competent hitter as soon as he put his mind to it.

The first step was to toss the ball up and swing the bat at it as it descended to the proper level. Just swing! Ah, but "that will take time," he thought, as he was unsuccessful in connecting the bat with the ball after about a dozen tries. Maybe, if he could get either his younger brother, who was a great ball player, or perhaps one of his buddies to pitch to him, he could concentrate more on the approaching ball, and he would be able to make the ball and bat connection.

His brother was only too glad to pitch to him and worked very hard pitching easy—no curves, fast balls or tricky maneuvers. It wasn't working. He concluded that his brother was too well experienced a ball player to be working well with a beginner such as himself. Perhaps one of his buddies, but which one? Trying to determine who was the least capable ball player he knew would have to be handled very carefully, lest he convey any impression that they were being asked because they were almost as poor at playing ball as it seemed he was. He settled on a friend who worked part-time with him in a department store and proceeded to ask him to pitch to him on some upcoming weekend.

Willingly, the friend showed up and proved that he was a far better pitcher than expected. Why wouldn't the connection come about? It was becoming obvious that there was more to hitting a ball with a bat than just imaging it. Was it time to concede?

The realization came; the conclusion was very clearly seen.

If the equipment could be somewhat modified to fit the situation, this could be the very solution.

Attached to the hitting end of the bat will be a double-strengthened tennis racket. Substituting for the softball that had been used in the failed practice sessions will be a basketball.

If this sounds like pure and simple nonsense, well it's no more nonsensical than expecting that repeated viewing of oneself in a photo posing with a baseball bat will result in becoming a great ballplayer.

ॐ

The sound of raindrops,
Like the rhythm of music
Falling on green leaves.

*****

Raindrops fall on leaves
Thunder in the far distance,
Hot afternoon breeze.
                    -M.T. Knight

The Man in the Moon
Sandy Jasnau

As a child, my dad would entertain me occasionally with a story of getting on a magic carpet and riding up to the moon where I would be entertained by **The Man in the Moon** with all kinds of childhood fantasies. So, naturally, when I became a mother and grandmother, I passed these stories on to my offspring. If one of them was experiencing a problem, this story offered a calming solution.

Back when my two little granddaughters started kindergarten together, however, this story took on a frightening twist. About the second day of school, Emily and Carissa failed to arrive at their daycare center after school. The school bus whizzed on by Ms. Kim's daycare without depositing my two little bundles of joy.

Well, as you can imagine, we adults, with our wild imaginations, went into overdrive. Ms. Kim called the school. The school called Grandma Sandy. Sandy called Terri, the mother of Emily and our son Robbie, the father of Carissa. And we burned up the telephone wires. Terri, who managed the Goodwill Store in Milledgeville, had all the customers praying in a circle at the store while Grandma Sandy was on the phone with son Robbie and the school.

After about three hours, the school was able to contact the school bus driver who had parked the bus for the evening. Upon checking the bus, there on the back seat were two little girls just waking up from their magical trip on the big, long, yellow magic carpet to the moon where they had been having a wonderful time with **The Man in the Moon**, and they were very happy and content with their escapade.

John-Thomas, My Grandson
Mary B. Purcell

His first word was "no;"
Not mama, dada, or run,
Which we should have done!

ℰᎧᏝ

The silent flower
With sweet fragrance in the air,
It speaks so loudly.
              -M.T. Knight

*****

Dawn of the morning
Comes first light of a new day,
Fills me with much joy.
              -M.T. Knight

*****

Peace is wonderful
The tranquil sound of silence,
Takes my breath away.
              -M.T. Knight

Grandma's Pastel Lace
Susan Lindsley

Spring is turning all the trees into a pastel lace
That brings to mind the ones that Grandma made when yesterplace
Was home and everything within the house was made by hand
And Grandpa only had a single mule to help him work the land.

But I always loved to ride with him upon the rake to gather up the hay
In windrows that he later piled in shocks against the rainy day.

And I remember how I felt that I was such a fool
The first time that my Grandpa sent me out alone to hitch the mule
Up to the wagon for us all to go to town,
For I forgot the trace chains and the wagon shafts just fell onto the ground
When Gracie took a step and left the wagon standing there.

And oh, how well do I remember what aromas filled the air
When Grandma fried up chicken and made her biscuits and her cake
For us to have an evening picnic and go fishing at the lake
Where all we ever caught would be a perch or two.
But anytime we caught too few
To bother taking home, Grandma showed us how to cook them in a special
         way,
To pack them in a coat of Georgia clay
And lay them in the coals as soon as flames were dying down.
And when the clay was cracking, dry and brown,
We'd take them from the coals and let them cool, then peel the fish
And eat them with our hands—we never bothered with a fork or dish.

What memories has the morning stirred of yesterplace
Because the trees reminded me of Grandma's home and all her tatting and the
         curtains she had made of pastel lace.

The Diet
Harriett Davis

For most of my adult life, I, like many of you, have been in denial. And like you, I had a multitude of reasons to justify my refusal to face reality. Reasons like, "I've got gland problems, slow metabolism, fat runs in my family, the scales lied, if God had meant for me to touch my toes He would have put them on my knees." I used every excuse in the book to keep from dieting.

I justified my size with this statement, I'm big boned. Natalie, my ex best friend, proceeded to grab my wrist, showing me how thin it really was. I wasn't fazed. Then she went too far. She pulled up my pants exposing my leg. I reminded her, I was a thoroughbred. Only plow horses had big legs. She reminded me, big legs went with big bodies and pencil stick legs went under slim bodies. Natalie had just called me fat; she had crossed the line. That's when she became my ex best friend. I was never going to speak to her again.

That night, I ate everything in the house. I had to build up my energy level for the diet. I wasn't that big. I calculated I only needed to lose five pounds. So I cut off all my hair. I took a water pill, three Fenament, three Correctols, and two Ex-laxs. I was serious. But all I lost that week was the time I spent in the bathroom. I gained two pounds. Go figure. Then it came to me, walking, that had to be the key to weight loss. But I needed to sweat too. So I rolled myself in Saran Wrap and started my walk. My court date for indecent exposure is next week. How was I to know to put my clothes back on over the Saran Wrap.

The next day, I sat at my kitchen table trying to formulate a fat attack plan. But some ingrate, ignorant of the world's state of famine, had left out eight pork chops, a pot of rice and gravy, a pan of corn bread, some collards cooked in fat back, and a pan of macaroni and cheese. I couldn't let that food go to waste, so I ate it...all. Then it hit me, water's the clue to weight loss. So I drank two glasses. I gained five pounds. Who knew water had hidden calories?

It was time to get serious. I left home jogging, all my clothes on this time. I passed the donut shop; I ate nine donuts. I passed the Dairy Queen; I ingested half a gallon of ice cream. Was I greedy? No, ice cream had eggs and milk. I needed the protein and calcium for my bone density. Now, my mom, God rest her soul, taught us against prejudice. She wouldn't want me to leave anyone out, so as I passed Rob's Rib

Shack, I ordered and ate a slab of ribs. Mom would have been proud of my principles.

Whoever said jogging was the key lied. I was up eleven pounds, I couldn't figure it out. Disgusted, I took to my bed. But I had a nightmare. I dreamed calories were in the air I was breathing. Grams of fat were stalking me. Pound after pound savagely pounced upon me. I tried to defend myself. I woke up with a new outlook and a new attitude concerning this weight loss thing. I came to three conclusions: I'm past my prime, and, at my age, thin ain't in; I need cushioning in case I fall. I must be one of those women meant to be big and beautiful; and you can't improve on perfection.

That settled, I sat down to a sensible meal of Ding Dongs, Polish sausages, a honey baked ham, crackling cornbread, scalloped potatoes, string beans, squash casserole, fresh corn, pasta salad, a half dozen deviled eggs, a chocolate cake—and to show my sincerity towards sticking to this diet, I drank a two-liter Diet Coke. After all, I was seriously cutting back.

ℰⓇⓒⓡ

Serene and peaceful
The cat naps on the soft chair,
Unaware of time.

-M.T. Knight

Aging Gracefully
or
How I Came to Grips With Support Hose
Margaret Ann Daniel

The latest adventure in my glorious journey to wisdom began when I went for a routine physical and my doctor asked me why I wasn't wearing support hose.

What! Me? Be one of those little old ladies wearing a hair net and walking around in stockings rolled down below her knees? How can a person possibly look cute in support hose?

"No one has ever told me to," I said.

"I'm telling you to," he said.

He told me why I needed them and that he would send me somewhere to be measured if I couldn't find any short enough.

I was not at all encouraged by what the local pharmacies offered.

There were tall black socks for men and queen-sized hose for women.

While it is true that I am the Queen of Me, and that I can be a drama queen at times, I knew that that was not exactly what the description meant.

Undaunted, and determined to learn how to find stuff on the internet, I logged on and Googled.

There, in the confusion, was a brand that I knew from my previous life, when the company I worked for insured the manufacturer.

I clicked on and got a picture of a really hot babe with long slim legs who had on four-inch stiletto heels and who looked confident and at ease.

Wow, if support hose will make me look that good, bring them on.

I studied the choices and typed my questions and sent them through.

A nice young man called and told me, no, they wouldn't have petite-sized ones until August and asked me to measure around my ankles and calves and from my feet to my knees while he waited.

I did, and he said that the smalls would probably work, but if they were too long, I could roll them down at the knees.

Since I needed them now, not August, I ordered three pairs to get free shipping and to save a few bucks in taxes by buying over the net.

They came a few days later, complete with an instruction sheet titled "Life With Compression Stockings" and a subsection titled "Instructions for Donning." It even told me that donning meant putting on and that wearing them might take some adjustment.

It spoke of powder—use it—and lotion—don't use it—and rubber gloves to assist in the donning and gripping.

It said to fold the top of the sock down over the foot of the sock and then to put my foot in until it met resistance.

I knew I was in trouble when I couldn't get my hand far enough into the sock to start the folding. When I did manage to, I couldn't find the heel.

I dug on down into the package and found a pamphlet with chic young models on the front, all glamorous in compression stockings.

Then I found what I needed; a pamphlet with a MATURE couple with white hair, smiling broadly with old teeth and dressed in colorful jogging suits. They were poised in mid-stride of a slow jog down a beach with the ocean in the background, having a great time and affording to live by the sea.

Written in the sand beneath them was Wearing Compression Garments Has Never Been Easier.

This pamphlet told me to start a new habit and gave me its own donning tips, including the caution that rolling or bunching or gathering up the fabric would make it feel like trying to stretch 100 rubber bands.

Among the donning methods was the heel-pocket method—forget that, I'd already lost one heel; the easy-slide method, which involved ordering something that looked like a big shoe horn and which required putting the bright green loop at the top of your foot and the pink loop at the bottom. For a person who has to reread the instructions every 6 months to change the time on the clock radio, this was too much.

My all-time favorite was the use of the Stocking Donner, a contraption that looked like a walker turned upside down, only smaller, and also available through the stocking company.

You were supposed to open the hose, stretch them over a thing in the frame of the donner and pull them more open, and presto, step right in and glide them up. Assuming you could get them open in the first place.

Having studied, underlined and highlighted all of the various methods, I finally stopped stalling and started over.

As soon as I began, my dog tried to grab them and run, as he does with my socks, but at $31 a pair, I thought not.

I got them on, donned my Birkenstocks, and sallied forth.

I visited my aunt, who told me I looked just like a lady we know who wears socks with sandals.

And lord, were they hot for a Georgia summer! I went back to the Net and ordered some without toes. They remind me of the leggings that ballerinas wear, and I always wanted to be a ballerina. And they are cooler.

I learned a lot from this experience.

I do not have to buy a contraption that looks like a vise for stretching and jumping into.

I just grab them, pull them on, and go on my merry way.

Rolling them down at the knees creates the 100 rubber bands effect, so I don't do it. But hey, I'm ready with a great tourniquet if I ever meet up with anybody who needs one.

As to looks—I won't be tall and skinny and glamorous. I'll look like me.

Anyway, if I listen attentively to you and focus on what you are all about, you won't even notice what I have on.

As a wise lady once said, "In time, your looks go. That's when you fall back on character."

∞⌘

The Temple*
Susan Lindsley

I saw in the Temple of Morning a light come out of the east
Into the pulpit of heaven in the crimson robes of a priest;

And from the Temple of Morning where all of life was begun
I looked at the Light that was rising and thought it was only the sun;

But someone was there in the temple, a priest or a holy someone,
Who whispered to me in the morning and said that the Light's not the sun;

"The Light that you see there is Holy and created you and the Son
And leads you forever from Darkness, so kneel now and pray to the One
Who gave you the Temple of Morning and gave you the Light of the Day."
So there with the one who was holy, I knelt in the temple to pray.

*In memory of my father's "The Temple of Morning."

Over Rated
Shane Riner

For all that's clear
With all I can't see
For all we made slip away
To think that
If I must go
To leave the sanctuary
Of your heart
That which is written
That which is thought
There is no more darkness
No more breath
No more steps to watch
No star to behold
The years we made
The final steps we crossed
That which shall be
No more

☙❧

Little hummingbird
Floating above the flowers,
Simply magical.
                    -M.T. Knight

Van Gogh Still-Life
Mary B. Purcell

Previously published:
Mary Binnicker Purcell, "Van Gogh Still-Life," *The Peacock's Feet,* Vol. 18, No. 1, Spring (1993): 38.

The paints screamed across the canvas
crashing browns and olives into
a seizure of noise and motion;
kicking, then rolling stiff-starch circles,
the colors tore away from one another,
shredding into shimmering fragments
which are contained within a frame
but are not content to hang on a wall.

ഈ)ൽ

Outside Myself
Patricia Byrd

I step outside myself to view
This process I'm advancing through
To be healed of inner strife
And learn of a richer life.

I may even say
My psyche is this way
Because of certain wrongs,
But this feat I could never perform alone.

Seventeen
Minnie Hamilton (Mallinson)

*This poem was written in 1944 and one of the "wondrous things to be"
was standing beside me in the woods; two years later we were married.*

It's good to be alive

To feel the wind blow through your hair,

To see the dusky twilight sky,

To hear the lonely wild bird's cry,

To smell the breath of burning leaves

On crispy autumn air;

It's good to be alive

To laugh with heart that's young and free,

To run with light step, unafraid,

To watch the sunset colors fade,

To gaze with dreamy eyes of youth

On wondrous things to be.

Stories From the Front Porch
Geloria Phelps

Sara and her two sisters were born and raised in a small rural farming town in Northeast Georgia in the late 1950's. They lived in a community called Apalachee Bridge. The landscape in this community was filled with pine trees, hardwood trees, red soil, and rolling hills. Families in this community grew cotton, corn, wheat, gardens, cows, pigs, chickens, and small children.

In the summer when the farms had been laid-by until time to harvest, Sara and her two sisters, who were in their early teens, would head down the red dirt road to their grandmother's house. Their grandmother lived alone in a white frame house near the road. The house had a front porch that stretched the width of the entire house. The porch was lined with flower pots filled with blooming and green plants. The containers that held the flowers were old discarded pots and pans that had sprung a leak and were no longer used for cooking in the kitchen. Occasionally, you would see an old white chamber pot in the mix. The yards had been swept neat and clean with a brush broom made from green dogwood trees. The broom had been cut down and tied with strings.

Seated in a cane bottom chair was a stately lady about six feet tall and weighing 190 pounds. Her hair was long, straight, and gray. Her hair was always neatly arranged. She would plait her hair in one long braid, which was pulled back and pinned up with a small ivory comb. She was 92 years old. Her skin was olive, and her nose was shaped like a Cherokee Indian Chief. She had most of her original teeth, even though they had been worn down a bit. There was a twinkle in her eyes that always made you think that she was up to some mischief. She wore a long print dress covered with a long white apron with two pockets in the front. Her legs were covered in cotton stockings, and she wore black leather high-topped shoes. This lovely lady was "Mo Erma," their grandmother.

When the girls found her seated on the porch in her chair, they knew that they were going to hear some stories about her past life. They would get excited! Mo Erma had a low convincing voice that made you want to listen to her. She always spoke with authority; you see, she had once taught school, even though she had very little formal education. Mo Erma would take her box of Tube Rose snuff along with her toothbrush out of her pocket. The toothbrush was made from a twig that came off a sweet gum tree in her front yard. One end of the twig had been chewed to form a brush. Mo Erma would open her snuff and dip her toothbrush into her snuff and place some of the snuff into her mouth. She would brush her teeth with her toothbrush and smile as she enjoyed the euphoria that came from the taste of her snuff. Mo Erma was now ready to use her white enamel spittoon on the right side of her chair and filled with sand. She was ready to tell some stories about her past life.

This particular day, she started by telling them about the Sunday her granddaughters came to visit her. Her granddaughters were sitting on her front porch enjoying themselves, while the adults remained inside the house. The large white house that she lived in at the time was owned by a white man who was her landlord. While her granddaughters were on the porch, they saw a cart pulled by two large steers, loaded with boys coming down the road in front of her house. The boys started calling her granddaughters' names. The girls ran into the house and told Mo Erma what had happened. She told them to go back and sit on the porch. She knew that the boys would have to come back up the road on their way home.

Meanwhile, Mo Erma peeped out of the small glass windows that were located on each side of the front door. Her granddaughters saw the boys coming back up the road on the cart drawn by two large steers. When they saw the girls on the porch, they started calling them names again. Mo Erma stepped out from behind the door and gave the boys a tongue lashing like they had probably never had before, especially from an old Negro lady. She told the boys that they should be ashamed of themselves for disrespecting her girls, and that she was going to tell their parents, or "folks" as she called them. The boys got scared and started whipping up the steers to make them go faster and were soon out of sight.

This was quite a feat for Mo Erma, especially since she was living in a house owned by parents of one of the boys who were on the cart, and since lynching was still taking place in the South during this time. However, no harm ever came to Mo Erma, and she did tell the boys' parents. Mo Erma thought that you should always stand up for what you believed to be right. From that time forward, her granddaughters would sit on her porch and were never bothered again.

Mo Erma was a religious lady who believed in going to church on Sundays and in helping her neighbors. She told them about the time she had gone down to the spring below her house to get water for her family. She saw a man who lived in the community named Rueben. He was cutting firewood in the forest. Rueben had a reputation for drinking liquor and carousing with the women. Mo Erma felt that this was the perfect time to help God out and save Rueben's soul. Rueben had not seen Mo Erma come to the spring. She stepped behind a large oak tree so that he could not see her and called out, "Rueben, go preach." She said that Rueben stopped cutting wood and listened, then started back cutting wood. She called out several more times, "Rueben, go preach." Eventually, Rueben left the forest, and she returned home. Mo Erma said she expected to hear that Rueben had started preaching, but she never did. Mo Erma said she did not have any remorse for playing God, but she now understood what a hard job God had. She smiled, and a twinkle came to her eyes.

Sara and her sisters realized that it was getting late, and they would soon be getting a call from their parents to come home. However, they wanted to hear more stories from Mo Erma. They begged Mo Erma to tell them about the time her son-in-law and her daughter were living with her and her family. You see, they had to stay there until they could find a place of their own to live. She said her son-in-law was very selfish. One day he brought home some sweet potatoes from his job and asked her to bake him a sweet potato pie. He told her that he was going to eat it all by himself. Mo Erma proceeded to prepare the sweet potato pie for him. That night she placed the pie along with the rest of the meal on the table for her family. When her son-in-law finished his meal, he reached for a slice of pie. He tasted it and was amazed when he realized that the pie tasted funny. Mo Erma had prepared the pie without using any butter, sugar, milk, eggs, or spices. Mo Erma said that she wanted to show him how selfish he was, living in her house and not being willing to share his pie with the rest of the family. She said her son-in-law did not learn too much from the pie experience, since he later brought home a bag of pecans and hid them from the rest of the family.

One day when she was cleaning house, she ran across the pecans and she and her family ate every last one of them. She placed the shells back into the bag, tied it up, and put it back where she found it. When her son-in-law found the bag, he knew that Mo Erma was the culprit.

Sara and her sisters heard their mother calling them to come home. They bid Mo Erma goodbye and ran back up the red dirt road, laughing and talking about the stories that Mo Erma had told them. The girls did not realize that Mo Erma had secretly taught them some lessons of life through her stories. Mo Erma smiled, and a twinkle came to her eyes.

Limbo Day
Therry N. Deal

What a day
A limbo day
Lost in thought
Lost in naught
Lost in cares so full of woe
How know I which way to go?

Limbo Day
Limp along
Caught in a funnel
    So large and strong
Limbo day, sure want to play
But vortex pulls the
    Joie away.

Limbo Day, do you last long?
Will twenty four hours
    Bring up a song?
Can Limbo day be just
    A dream
And blue sky day be the
    Cat's cream?

Oh, Limbo Day—go far away!

Murmuring Pines
Patricia Byrd

Our pines are murmuring softly among themselves—
Those same ones that were raging, releasing their
Debris upon the earth.
We are like that, murmuring gently one day,
Raging the next and even posing serenely on another.

Just as it would not seem right
For the trees always to be the same,
Our souls need the changes, however painful,
That come to compare, to balance, to give us
A sense of real life.

 howQ

Christmas Sick
Doyle Boyd

The sociopaths failed Christmas –

All of them flunked:

Too many spirits

And they ended up drunk.

Where Have the Years Gone?
"The Early Years"
Martha J. Williams

It seems as if the years have sped by and the events in my life have slowed down. I am now in my fifties, but my mind tells me that I am much younger. This is not a bad state of mind since I can remember events that have occurred in my life as if they happened a few years ago. The mind is an amazing thing. Thank God that I can still remember things as if I am reliving them over and over in my mind.

The best way to have my mind catch up with my chronological age is to record as many memories from my past as possible. Some of these memories were pleasant, some funny, some motivational, and some tragic. I believe that each of us has events during our life to help us become who we are.

I can remember back to the time I was two or three years old. My family lived in a small town in Alabama just outside of Selma. Our small house was located just through a path close to my grandmother's house. I can remember visiting her all of the time. There were other children at Mama's house, but I can remember only my mother, my father, and me living at our house.

I can remember the trees that surrounded our house. They were fruit and nut trees. My mother would take the fruit from these trees and make delicious jams and jellies from them. I can remember her cracking the nuts and feeding the meat inside to the other children from Mama's house and me. I was confused about who these children were, but I was glad that I had someone to play with all the time.

My mother would sit in a cane bottom chair either in the front yard or on the front porch of our small house. She would rock back and forth in that chair all the time. I also remember that my father worked in the fields until noon each day. When he came home, Mother would have an empty syrup can that she used for his lunch. He would get the can and then go back to the fields. No matter how hard he worked he always made time to play marbles with me for a few minutes. My hands were too small to shoot marbles, but he always made me feel like I was the winner of the game. After returning from the fields, he chopped wood so that my mother could wash clothes or cook for us.

I cannot remember what the inside of our house looked like, or what furniture we had in it. I just remember the inside of the house being dark most of the time. I suppose that was why we spent a lot of time outside in the yard, or at Mama's house. There was a big black pot sitting in the yard near our house. Mother used that pot to boil our sheets, or to make lye soap in every week. Come to think of it, all the other houses that we visited had a black pot outside of their houses, too. I guess everybody in Alabama had a black pot they used for making soap and washing clothes. When my mother was not using the pot, I would use it as a toy. I can remember getting dirty from all the "black stuff" that was on the outside of the pot. I later learned that that black stuff was called soot.

One day my parents were fussing about something. They woke me up. I was scared. I remember grabbing my bottle with a nipple on top, and my sack doll and walking away from the house. I can remember wearing a piece from a large flour sack as underwear and no shoes on my feet. I had blisters and bug bites all over my legs. Although I was young, I knew that I had to make it to Mama's house. There I would be with the other children and be safe. When I reached Mama's house, I crawled up in a large rocking chair and rocked myself to sleep.

I don't know how long I was there, but I do remember hearing Mama telling my parents to let me sleep. She wanted to know how I got in the house without anyone seeing me. She was angry at her daughter, my mother, for scaring me to the point that I had to run away from home. Neither of my parents said a word. Back in those days, Mama was in charge of all of her children and grandchildren. They all gave her respect. She told them that I would stay with her until I felt safe enough to return home. I moved into Mama's house and stayed for a long time. While living there, I learned that the other children at her house were hers. They were her third set of children from her third husband. They were my aunts and uncles.

My uncle Edward and my aunts Ernestine and Lucinda became my best friends. I enjoyed being around them. Edward was five years older than I, so we played together more than my aunts and I because they were much older. I visited my parents all the time, but I didn't stay with them much. I guess you can say that I lived with a foster mother, who was my grandmother. This arrangement lasted for one year. That's when I learned that my mother was going to have a baby. I knew that everything was about to change. I would have another child in our small house. In addition to my uncle and aunts, I would have my very own person to take care of, play with, and love.

Bouncing in the Billows
Minnie Hamilton Mallison

Bouncing in the billows,

Frothing in the foam,

Lolling in the lulls between

'Til more combers come;

Buffeting the breakers,

Sputtering in the spray,

Oh, I could go on bobbing here

Forever and a day!

ഇഓൽ

A beautiful sight
Bluebird on my window sill,
I make three wishes.

-M.T. Knight

Friends – Past and Future
Evangeline Lundy

Hello Friend. My name is Chocolate Chip Boyd. My Father's name is Bernard B. Boyd. The Boyds are a very distinguished and well known family. I have been retired for a few years now. However I am on the scene and visible every day. Nevertheless, I am seldom noticed or spoken to these days. However, my thoughts are happy because I spend a lot of time remembering the good old days when my best friend, Amanda, and I entertained many famous guests. One of our favorite people was "Papa." He had big hands, with thick skin. He played golf a lot, and I saw him many times with a golf club in his hands. But when we served him tea and cookies in our fine, real hand-painted porcelain china, his touch became delicate and even graceful. He seemed to enjoy our picnics more than any of our other guests, so we always especially enjoyed serving him. I think we must have poured out gallons of tea for him to drink. Maybe part of his enjoyment came from the fact that the tea set was carefully hand-painted by our cousin "Pinky." She is a very talented artist. She has her own kiln that she uses to "fire" the porcelain. She made matching napkins, and picnic cloth and other accessories. She added a book by a famous author. The final touch she added to the presentation was Chocolate Chip Boyd—that's me!! The sets are difficult to make and so Pinky made only a few each year. The sets are so rare that they are sold only in specialty shops where wealthy people are happy to pay over $400.00 to own one.

Yes, I do miss our "glory days of the past." However, I must admit that I now occupy a position of honor, even though I am no longer active. I have time to relive the happy memories. In fact, I cherish them. And even though "Papa" is gone now, I still see Amanda occasionally. I know that she loves me, and that she always will. I know in my mind and in my heart that the great days of happiness will be repeated. I will be with another devoted companion, who will probably be my beloved Amanda's child. In time there will be another circle of best friends to share the tea and cookies.

May I give you some important advice? You have have heard it before, written by Jimmy Kennedy and set to music:

*If you go down in the woods today you'd better not go
alone.*
It's lovely down in the wood today
But safer to stay at home.
For ev'ry Bear that ever there was
Will gather there for certain, because
*Today's the day that the Teddy Bears have their
picnic!!*

    Goodbye for now, I wish you the best of everything. I hope that you will have the good fortune that I have had. May you be loved always and forever by someone who has a pure heart and an innocence of my Amanda Lee. There is a season and a time for everything. My time will come again when the required circle of time has been completed.
    Your friend,
    Chocolate Chip Bear

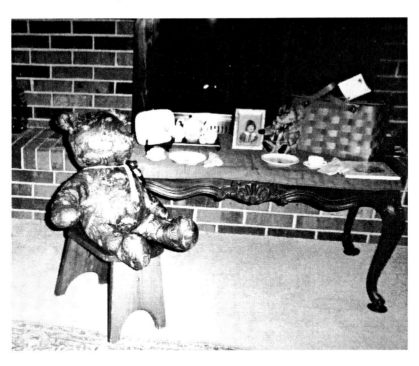

My Mother's Hands
Carrie Cox

My sisters and I often get together and recall the many talents our mother possessed and the countless ways she gave of herself. We fondly speak of those days right after the Great Depression in the Thirties and Forties when we were not aware that money was in short supply. Our Mama made our lives, as well as those around her, rich in love, compassion and generosity.

One of Mama's favorite sayings was "Idle hands are a devil's workshop," and certainly she was never content to sit idly by when her family was occupied elsewhere. She made her daily trip to the post office, one of her many community services. She wrote and took correspondence for merchants who could not leave their stores, and returned to them with whatever mail they had received. She spent time each morning with the aged and infirm who lived within walking distance, and with one neighbor who had a terminal illness and depended on her for Scripture readings and prayer.

Among my mother's varied talents was her ability to design and sew clothes. Whether it was from a picture or a verbal description, she

would cut her own pattern from newspapers, fit it to us, then make the designed fashion look like a department store purchase. I'm certain she could have made her mark in the competitive world as a designer, but thank goodness she decided against a professional career and modeled her clothes on us instead.

I modeled one of her most memorable fashions when I was but three years old. I was chosen from among community children to be a bridesmaid in a Tom Thumb Wedding at The City Elementary School. My memory does not serve me well enough to actually remember the play but OH HOW I REMEMBER THE DRESS MY MAMA MADE FOR ME. (I'm sure the feeling parallels that of Dolly Parton's remembrance of the Coat of Many Colors her mother made for her.) The proper costume was left up to the parents of the children and where some mothers would have panicked at not having the money to buy material, my mama simply bought a roll of pink crepe paper and let her creativity go to work. She made a bodice with narrow shoulder straps and sewed it onto a full-length skirt. Then she added fluted tiers made with her nimble fingers and her ever ready scissors. This gave the dress an attractive ruffled effect. The audience responded well when I walked on stage with my escort, George Echols. Later on when "It's Only a Paper Moon" was being sung everywhere, we could almost believe Mama made and hung it.

Born with a love of music, my mama taught us songs from every decade. One of the first things she had us learn was the books of the Bible as a song. They have remained easily in our minds to this day. Folk songs, love songs, every hymn—she knew them all. With no formal music training, she played the piano as well as many stringed instruments such as the mandolin, ukulele, and guitar. She was also an accomplished violinist.

She spent many hours each week addressing cards to the sick and shut-in. Somehow, she knew them all. She had a notebook filled with names and birthdays, completed with current addresses of those who had moved elsewhere. She was faithful to send these greetings to all.

Any gathering attended by Mama's children, i.e., reunions, weddings, and her name is sure to be mentioned with affection by others who knew and remember her. At a recent Midway School reunion breakfast, one of the men recalled to me how my mama had been a leader of a Boy Scout Troop and that she had done a very capable job. This same troop was involved in collecting newspapers for the WW II war effort, and since there was no central repository Mama allowed the papers to be stacked on her porch. One by one, the now 75-year-old Boy Scouts came up to me and spoke of how they still remember, with great fondness, my mama.

Several years back, I received a letter from a missionary to Japan who was taking a sabbatical in Augusta, GA. Somehow she obtained my address and wrote, wanting me to know that my mother was responsible for her finding Christ at a very young age when she attended a class my mother taught in Sunday School. This lady had a very unhappy home life and was being reared by her grandparents. They walked with her about two miles on Sunday mornings to attend Sunday School and church and the impression my mother made on her young life enabled her to overcome her background, and she has gone on to reach and teach many others in her lifetime.

Adaptable hands. Capable hands. She never used hand creams and seldom polished her nails, but her hands were beautiful. I once read of a poor, elderly lady who, on her deathbed, lamented that she had nothing to take to the Lord. Someone who knew she had lived to do for others said to her, "Don't worry, just show Him your hands."

So, "Just show Him your hands, Mama."

ഇെരു

The Dancing Lady
Susan Lindsley

I saw a lady dancing down the sidewalk in my town,
Wearing a tiara and a red and purple gown.

She danced with twilight shadows in the circle of her arms,
And on her wrists and ankles she wore amulets and charms.

She danced as if to music with her rhythm and her swaying,
Like a lonely lover or a pagan woman praying.

On and on she danced alone, along the city street,
Until I felt the rhythm of her dancing in my feet.

When I joined the lady in the red and purple gown,
The street began to fill with all the people of the town.

Everyone was dancing with the rhythm and the beat
Of the silent music in the dancing lady's feet.

A Scented Story
Ed Bzdyk

Electronic media equipment, such as tape recorders, projectors, and record players had been unexplainably disappearing from the Special Services building at K-55 Osan Air Force Base, Korea. The situation was baffling air police at the base. Special Services personnel were immediately put under surveillance to determine culpability, but thus far, appeared to be quite innocent. Naturally, all vehicles departing base premises were regularly checked, but under the circumstances, more stringent inspection of trucks and jeeps was being ordered. Even the flight line was included in the inspection campaign. All outgoing aircraft were carefully checked over. It soon became evident that somehow, someway, the supply of equipment was still dwindling. Last but not least, the barbed-wire perimeter fences now were coming under watchful eyes, lest those testosterone laden lads were paying for favors out in the rice paddies with Special Services equipment.

One fine day, and I might add there were few in Korea, a couple of buddies and I signed out a jeep to take a ride into Seoul, Korea's capitol city. It was somewhat of an adventuresome trek inasmuch as the route was upon what we unaffectionately called Sygman Rhee's "Express Highway." It was strongly rumored that the trees lining the road from Osan to Seoul were acquired with funds from the United States, but for use in other areas of need. Nonetheless, there were trees aplenty decorating the route, but that did not really render the trip all that pleasant since the dirt surface of the "Highway" was designed by the same person who manufactured my grandmother's washboard. To add to this "bucolic" scene, the road cut through the rice paddy fields, which added a very distinct and constant odor. To better explain the smell that surrounded our entire trip, I will need to advise you of what element was used to fertilize the rice fields. More importantly, I need to tell you how the base personnel contributed to the farmer's acquisition of this specific fertilizer.

Facilities on the base for disposal of human waste were of the design to handle the situation quickly and efficiently. These facilities were not, however, similar to those found on Air Force Bases stateside, or at least not to my knowledge anyway. There were buildings which housed latrines, strategically placed to be shared by several Quonset huts. These structures were not of any special architectural value, but they more or less served their purpose. Those of you who are acquainted with the rural outhouses of years ago would probably find a similarity in what purpose the buildings served, but these latrines were definitely constructed to handle a good bit more traffic. As an example, I believe some outhouses were "two-holers," thus allowing pleasant conversation while taking care of nature's needs. The base latrines were eight-holers. Underneath the holes was a very wide trough at which one end was positioned a six-inch wide pipe with a valve. The trough was pitched downward from that pipe and ended at the other end of the building. At an appropriate time of the day—hopefully when the "holes" were not occupied—the valve was opened and the cascading torrent of water washed down the trough to the other end of the building. Fortunately, the man, who was affectionately referred to as "the honey bucket man," had containers properly positioned at the other end to receive the contents of the trough. Appropriately, these containers were called "honey buckets." We on the base, therefore, very willingly gave to the farmers that which was needed to fertilize the rice paddies.

Now, it just so happened that the day my buddies and I were just about to enter the outer limits of the city—ahead of us was our "honey bucket man" and his treasured cargo; we remained a respectful distance, as you can imagine that sniffing this particular stuff was enough when driving through the rice fields, but to approach the cart on which were hanging eight fully loaded buckets was too much for even the staunchest of airmen. It was fortuitous indeed that we kept a more than respectful distance because, as the "honey bucket cart" entered into the intersection, a good sized truck ran smack into the cart's midsection. I guess all of you probably wondered exactly what it would look like if you personally witnessed a happening where it was clear that the s—t flew. Well, let me tell you—it was beyond imagination.

Perhaps you are wondering what might be the connection between the earlier part of my story and this unfortunate accident? Well, the mystery of the missing equipment from Special Services was solved. Yep! You guessed it. Pieces of the equipment were secreted in the individual buckets, so when the s—t flew—so did the electronics.

The Old Woman and the Turkey
Susan Lindsley

Silent as her shadow, the old woman slipped from the darkness of her living room onto the porch that looked eastward, where a sliver of moon lay on its back above the still-naked persimmon at the edge of the hayfield.

Eighty-one is not too old to turkey hunt, she thought. Soon as I get my son fed and on the road, I'm going after Buster. That boy thinks I'm fragile as a china doll, but I'll show him I can still get about in the woods. He thinks if I get out of the house I'll hurt myself. "He's got another think coming," she vocalized.

She wanted one more turkey hunt, one more time to see spring spread itself out before her, one more time to hear the day awaken and the toms gobble from the pine ridge. One more time to show that son she didn't need to go to a nursing home. At least his vacation was over and if she woke him now, she could have him gone by sunup.

She wouldn't tell him her plans, seeing as how he would just throw a fit. But when she returned, she would tell the story of killing old Buster, the only wild turkey that earned a name, not only because he stood a foot higher than all the other toms, but also because for three years he'd made a fool of her son.

She'd call him tonight to tell him she had killed that bird when he had failed so many times. That would put an end to his talking about a nursing home.

She should have never stopped hunting. Maybe it was her Cherokee blood that lured her to the wilderness. For a moment she was back in the river swamps with her father, half-Indian, where he had taught her about turkeys and how to call them. He had made her a cedar box call, and she had used it until she finally had mastered his lessons on how to use just her vocal cords to "yoink" and "cluck" like a hen.

Her mind flashed from the swamps to the railroad, to the morning she and Billy walked home from what was their last hunt, the day he collapsed with a fatal heart attack and died while bringing home his turkey that spring morning.

So many changes since then. Even the railroad was closing down, the last train coming to town later today in a ceremonial run to bring the governor to town. Then the engine would become a local tourist sight. The abandoned tracks and the right of way would revert back to her family. As soon as she lay buried beside Billy, that boy of hers would bring even more changes, would turn the old railroad bed into a street, and would plant houses where the oaks and dogwoods now fed deer and turkey. She did not want to live to see the rails gone, those flowing silver ribbons that floated up and down over the soft places as the train roared by.

She would hunt just one more time, she'd head for the woods as soon as she got that boy up, fed, and off down the road to Atlanta.

Old Buster roosted on the ridge just above Big Creek, in the high pines about a hundred yards off the railroad, where dominate toms gobbled every spring morning since long before Billy fell dead between the rails.

Today she would use Billy's old single shot that had been in her closet since that day. How many years ago now? Only six, she realized, but their emptiness made them seem forever.

She would get that old Buster and show the boy she wasn't dead yet, and he would have to wait awhile before he could lock her away, tear up creation and pave over her world. She would show him she wasn't as old as he thought. You're not old until you forget and can't remember you've forgotten. She always remembered if she forgot something. Folks under sixty don't know about getting old. Old is only thinking old.

The distant song of a whip-poor-will shattered the silence as the condensation under the tin roof dripped coolness on her arm. She listened for any sound that might awaken Buster, as she had stood on the porch every spring since her son demanded she no longer hunt, no longer spend the silence of predawn in the woods, no longer see the birth of day and hear the earliest woodsongs out of sight and hearing of other humans. The woods weren't a lonely place, nowhere near as lonely as sitting in a crowd.

A pair of geese rolled overhead against the stars as they announced the approach of dawn. Buster gobbled, and the morning trembled.

"Humrpt" she grunted. "Still on that ridge." She went to wake her son, to start him on his long drive back to the city. She'd not tell him Molly wasn't coming back until tomorrow. As long as he expected Molly here today, he'd go home. She chuckled to herself for having sent her "keeper" off on a vacation for an extra day so she'd have some time for herself.

With promises to call her every evening after work, the boy drove off, his Caddie kicking yellow pollen and red dust high into the dew-moist dawn.

Moments later she pulled on her hunting clothes. The buckskin wore dark shadows from old sweat, and the tassels were long gone, but the pants and jacket fit her form that was as slim as 65 years ago. She reckoned she was shrinking again after putting on weight from inactivity after Billy died.

She broke the shotgun and looked down the barrel that gleamed from the last cleaning. From the overhead shelf, she took down the old box of shells, looked at the seven shells laid haphazardly inside. She removed only one, checked that it was a No. 2, and slipped it into the chamber of the old Stevens .12 gauge single shot. One turkey, one shot, she told herself.

She picked up the box call that she had chalked last night. The rag between the box and the striker kept it silent as she slipped it into a pocket.

At the fireplace, she reached into the cold chimney for soot and smeared it over her face and hands. With Billy's shotgun dangling from one hand, she left for Buster's ridge as dawn backlit the trees. She strode with the steady confident stride that had carried her across the swamps with her father a lifetime ago.

Late to start out on a turkey hunt, with the birds already on the ground. But any time of day is a good time to be out talking to turkeys.

Although slowed with her years, she was alive with adrenalin and with the passion of again being alone in the woods. She blended as a shadow blends against tree trunks, her worn buckskins becoming the shadows of leaves, trees, straw and vines, her white hair pushed under the plain brown cap that Billy had left hanging in the tool shed. She carried the shotgun lightly; compared with her iron skillets, the shotgun felt almost weightless. Her moccasined toes remembered to seek sticks before her weight fell onto each foot so no cracking stick alerted the woods. As she eased through the shadows, the restrictions imposed by her son and four walls slide away.

God, it's been a long time, she thought, emptying her mind of everything except the land around her, absorbing only what would take her to the wild turkey—the scratched leaves, the white-edged droppings beneath a pine that served as a roost. A gobbler's roost. She smiled, remembering how her father had shocked her mother when he explained to his 12-year-old daughter the difference in tom and hen droppings by comparing their shapes to those of male and female sexual organs.

As Buster consumed her thoughts, the spring around her faded— the dogwoods lifting white petals like prayers to the morning, the sunlight filtering through the new leaves to create a dreamworld of green, and the wild azaleas flooding pinks and yellows across the hardwood bottom.

When he gobbled, she froze while her mind analyzed direction and volume. He must be near the junction of the old cotton-wagon road and the railroad, close to 200 yards away.

She hurried northward and stayed away from the railroad, keeping behind thickets as she worked her way toward the crossing. When still 100 yards away, she stopped against a pine and listened. Five minutes became 10 and then 20 before Buster bellowed at the morning. Another gobbler echoed his call, and hens cackled back.

Looking for somewhere to hide, but no more than 30 yards from the railroad bed, she selected an oak twice as wide as her shoulders as a readymade backrest. In seconds, she kicked out a swale at its base, perched her bottom onto the soft mulch remaining, and tested the sitting comfort and the view. It would do. Rising, she kicked leaves away from where her feet would be. A pocketknife snipped off a tiny dogwood that would tremble with any movement she made. Can't have the plants talking to Buster, she thought. Sitting, she pulled the shotgun tight against her shoulder and swung it from side to side, ensuring that the scattered small pines and vines in front of her were far enough away not to impede movement. She quickly slashed down the one pine that flicked against the barrel and stuck the pointed end into the ground a foot farther away to maintain some cover. She settled down, her knees pulled up to provide a rest for her shotgun and to shield her hands in her lap as she worked her box call.

When old Buster got close, she would put the hand-held call on the ground, hold the shotgun at the ready, and coax him close by calling with only her vocal cords that she had kept in training over the years.

One series of "yoinks," so soft that only a turkey could hear it more than a few yards away, and Buster challenged the morning.

She waited. And waited. Would he move to meet the hen or demand that she come to him? Had her son gotten him call wise? Was her skill with the cedar call still good enough to fool even Buster?

He gobbled again. She gave another series of soft calls.

Silence.

Far in the distance the train whistled, and Buster answered. Must be at Dixon's Crossing, a good half-hour away.

Minutes seemed to be hours.

Then she saw him, a blob of black through the understory, far beyond the range of her 1913 Stevens single shot. The blob widened, enlarged, and became a semicircle that rotated one way and then back the other as Buster beckoned hens to his sunlit dance. Even at that distance the brilliant red of his head sent excitement surging through her. Buster *was* big.

Her heart rose into her throat, her pulse beat harder and harder until she tried to swallow. Her throat, filled with her heartbeat, didn't want to work. She gulped air, once, deeply, then again and again. The shotgun in her hands was shaking and heavy, her palms so wet they were slick. She wanted to rub her palms against the buckskin but knew she dared not move. The pulse in her throat rose into her head, pounded in her temples. Buster, as if he was aware of her reaction, dropped his tail, collapsed his strut, walked without concern along the tracks a few yards toward her and then erupted into another strut.

The old woman willed her body under control; the trembling stopped, her throat accepted a swallow, the shotgun became light.

Three other toms appeared, fanning their tails each time he fanned; when he gobbled, they answered from behind him. Knights to a king, yes men to a corporate commander, lieutenants to a general, they acknowledged Buster's command and dominance.

They moved toward her. Each time they swelled into a strut they carefully lifted one foot in her direction and then rotated in the slow courtship dance, with only each other and the old woman for an audience. The hens didn't show themselves if they were still behind the gobblers. Each time they dropped from strut, they walked two or three steps in her direction. Then they disappeared behind some thickets, still some 70 yards away.

She placed the box call on the ground. Too much calling had cost her several turkeys when she was young and impatient. Let him wonder and come looking.

Day moved forward faster than the birds, but the same patience that had kept her obedient to her son's demands now kept her body obedient to her mind as she willed herself to stay immobile. The toms would be close enough for her shot when they came back into sight. Mosquitoes found her; no-see-ums settled around her eyes, crawled into her ears, feasted on her hands. She felt something move down her collar and begin to sting her back, felt the feet of a tick crawling, but only her eyes moved, to blink away the insects. The charcoal on her face began to streak with the sweat of her tension; her hands, feeling the anticipation of her emotions, began to tremble and then steadied again as she pushed the tension down, turning her body away from it as she had turned away from the loneliness encroaching her after Billy's death. She took a deep breath, let it seep into her belly and lift her shoulders; she held it, savored it, and slowly released it into the cloud of insects gathering to feast on her unresisting body.

She merged into the tree and into the ground. Her backside felt a vine she had not kicked away somewhere beneath the mulch, almost a knife slicing into her flesh. Every wave and edge in the bark behind her bit into her back. Her fingers locked around the shotgun, her thumb locked down on the hammer, and she eased it back while pressing lightly on the trigger to cock it silently. With her left hand propped against her left knee to hold the barrel steady, she pulled the stock tight against her right shoulder and rested her cheek on the stained wood, ready for Buster to strut into range.

A jay squawked at the toms, and then silence seemed to approach as songbirds quieted ahead of the turkeys. The jay continued to scream and herald the toms while warning the rest of the world to silence. A two-year old tom strolled in front, stopped near the pine she'd figured to be 30 yards away. He swelled into a strut, threw out his fan, pulled his head close to his chest, closed his eyes as if in ecstasy, and slowly turned to show himself to whatever hens might be nearby. The morning sun caught bronzes, greens, and reds like a kaleidoscope, ever changing.

Behind him came another tom, and then another, all larger than those she remembered from years ago, their heads red, white, blue and massive, their beards almost touching the ground. Their spurs shone black when they lifted their feet in the ritual dance.

One by one they passed the pine tree, like a parade of prehistoric raptors, but Buster was not there. Mosquitoes dug into her hands and face; no-see-ums delighted in an air dance before her eyes; her back throbbed; her legs ached; her hands went numb. She did not move.

Aware that a turkey could see her eyes blink at 50 yards, she squinted to keep from blinking.

Buster appeared, his head curled against his flared feathers, his tail spread like a fan across the horizon; his double beard dragged the crossties and gravel, his wings scratched loudly against wood and rocks, his waddle redder than blood throbbed with sexual excitement and anticipation. His drumming rolled to her, as loud as a dozen cats purring against her chest.

Oblivious to everything but himself, Buster strutted into her line of fire. She trembled as a warmth spread over her, the power of life and death, the need for taking this trophy of all trophies, the reality that here before her stood her only hope of escaping the nursing home.

Her heart hammered in her throat so loudly she knew he could hear as she breathed in all the way to her belly, slowly let the air out, swallowed once to moisten her throat. She had to pull Buster from his strut to have a target—no way she would take a chance on shooting him in full strut and only injuring him.

She "yoinked" once.

Buster's head shot up from his strut, his waddle almost exploding with red, his eyes expectant, searching, hopeful, anticipating.

She held the bead solidly on the blood-red waddle, eased her thumb off the hammer, and squeezed slowly down on the trigger. She gave no thought to the frailty of her body or the power of the shotgun's kick.

Her follow-through as natural as a ball player letting his hand keep flowing to ensure accuracy, she kept the gun steady-on after the explosion. When she saw feathers flying, she pulled the shotgun down and rose to her feet, all in one continuous motion, her body forgetting age and its creaking joints. She leaped forward, ready to claim her trophy.

On her fourth step, with the whistle of the governor's train blaring, she stepped into a stump hole and heard the crack as her leg broke. She began the long fall into the ditch, aware only of the train bearing down on the body of Buster lying in splendor between the rails.

⁊ʃɢ

Tired Reindeer
Doyle Boyd

Up on the housetops
Reindeer crawled...
They had finished their tours
With spiked drinks that were tall.

Angels Hate
Shane Riner

I ask for no lonely day,
Just peace of mind not to be noticed.
I don't want death,
Just the future to be untainted.
I will not be banned.
I will not be punished.
I, who have lost at love yet once more,
Would die for no reason. Let human existence
Make time end;
Let hell freeze over.
I'll never miss the day...
The day that I die
With you.

Patience
Mary Binnicker Purcell

Early each morning the grey heron stands on the point overlooking the Oconee River. I see him from my kitchen window, where I sit, drinking my tea, balancing my checkbook and my life.

Patience. He seems a statue, but I have seen his dark eyes and lithe movements.

Patience. The necessities of life are within his reach—food and water. He knows, as do I, that the strike of his bill, almost unseen, will net his prey; there is no escape. And what am I learning?

Patience. If you rush through life, you miss more than you gain from your experiences.

Patience. Always keep your eyes on the prize.

Patience. The goal is Obtainable!

Epworth Night
Therry N. Deal

So silently across the night sky waft the cadre of geese.
Only a chance moment—a look upward lets me spy.
Was that God's gentle sign of promise that lifted my eyes?

The geese know not where they go—but they know they must
And so—they fly.
Each year the steady cycle of their being creates a rhythm of
Life that lifts them on wing.
And man?—we fight the inevitable facts of time.
No sensuous pages of direction have we—
Sometimes warring with kith or kin or foe.
For what purpose man?
Why not the steady cycle of life set to the human rhythm which
Gives it sustenance?

And I? Can I yield to the steady rhythm of life?
This dark night is still, yet alive, and I am part of it.
It is not the dark night of goodbye—it is the soft night of
"hello."

So go silently wild geese, and thus set a path for me that
I may listen to the sound of soft darkness knowing a morn is
Somewhere and yet lit by the SON!

This Is Our Life
Patricia Byrd

This is our life going by;
This is the winter almost gone.
I think on these things as I see the leaves fly.
These are the days we should cherish,
Moment by moment.
This is our life going by;
Let us count it as a blessing.
Let us make memories we can treasure.

Back in Teheran
After My Mother's Death in My Absence
Barry Darugar

I walk in the roofed bazaar, rays
filter through diamond-
shaped windows and light—
tiny dust spheres:
Invading starships
from galaxies afar.
In corners of mud-brick
walls spooky shadows lurk.
From far off, the clang of iron,
hammer of copper plates,
and chants of produce vendors
form a Scheherazade
melody of my childhood.

Butcher shops with slabs of beef
hung from the ceiling hooks,
the fruit carts full
of pomegranate, mulberry, and apricot,
by the *joob,* bakery
with *sangak* bread that slopes
down from *tanoor's* inferno
hot pebbles imbedded
In bread I had to juggle
In my eight year old hands
taking to a breakfast
of cheese, *chaii,* with a lump of sugar.

Goats, camels, and mules lumber
by, their sounds harmonize with
the symphony of Teheran's
Bazaar. I walk farther
down to Ferdowsi's Garden.
The air is redolent with jasmine
her favorite cologne. I
feel my mother's presence.
Her gentle dark eyes framed
In tresses of hennaed hair.

Her gaze warms my face
I say, "I'll never leave you."
She asks, "When did you return?"
Her eyes cloud. I turn
my face away—farther than I
expected, longer than I wanted.
Even though, I'm back
Here now, yet without her
the emptiness
Lingers—longer and deeper
like the golden rays
Penetrating the inner
Sanctum of the old Bazaar.

ॐ

So Far Away in Time
Susan Lindsley

Memories, like an army, march forever in my soul,
Taking me to Milledgeville when I was 10 years old.

To the days the train would smoke its way along the street,
When an open fireplace was our only source of heat.

To the days before you had to earn both wealth and fame
For everyone in town to know your family and your name.

To the days the Jessies came to teach at PHS,
And schools required that every girl should always wear a dress.

To the days the picture show would cost a child a dime.
So far away that Milledgeville—so far away in time.

A Special Gift
Martha Chandler Tomlin

"What-cha-doin'?" I asked. I was visiting with Mr. Sam, he was my daddy's ginner at Brown's Crossing. If it were a slow day for cotton, Mr. Sam would spend spare afternoon hours working on a wood project of his own choosing. Occasionally, I could visit him on the second floor of the gin house where he had a small workbench.

"I'm making a surprise for you." he declared.

"You're just making another old washboard; that's all you ever make. I don't want a washboard." This scene repeated itself many times; Mr. Sam would smile and never share his secret.

At last my surprise was finished and under the tree at Christmas; it was a log cabin doll house! The outside walls were grooved to resemble logs. The two windows and door were wood and opened with tiny wooden hinges. The front steps were two round circles cut from a tree limb. There was a chimney carefully grooved to resemble individual bricks. The roof was designed with shingles; one side lifted up to gain access to the room below.

This was the era before plastic furniture. Thanks to Santa Claus, MY log cabin came with REAL furniture. There were twin beds with blue spreads, a bedside table with gold-painted lamp, and a chest with drawers which really opened. There was a round table with four chairs and a rocking chair to sit by the fire and knit.

This doll house gave me many hours of pleasure. It was home for my doll family. I made curtains from scraps and hung them with thumb tacks on straw rods.

Perhaps the most amazing part of this story is this special gift was designed and made by Mr. Sam, a bachelor who lived with his maiden sister in a large two-story house in the community. It was not the washboard I had expected but the special log cabin made for ME.

&)C&

My serenity:
Sitting on the porch alone,
I am not lonely.
                    -*M.T. Knight*

Why I Don't Do Mail Order
Margaret Ann Daniel

People who like to order merchandise by mail tend to hold forth at great length with examples of convenience and time saved by their preferred shopping method.

I've always been leery of mail order, fearing that the ordered item wouldn't fit or that I wouldn't like it. Nor did I want the hassle of repacking something and sending it back.

A year ago, I succumbed to temptation when I got yet another fat envelope stuffed with colorful slips of paper with pictures of wonderful non-essential items on both sides.

I took a Last Chance to Order offer of a manual typewriter for only $66, plus $18 for three boxes of ribbons, plus $3 for handling, for a grand total of $90.

After copying the required stock numbers carefully into the little boxes on the order blank, writing in "portable manual typewriter" in the description block, and enclosing a photocopy of the item I wanted, I rushed my order off to California.

I was really excited three weeks later when the mailman delivered my package, though I was surprised at how heavy it was.

It wasn't at all heavy for a box of six claw hammers, each weighing 16 ounces, along with three boxes of typewriter ribbons.

A quick check of the paperwork showed that sure enough, I wrote one incorrect digit, and that, by golly, despite the correct verbal description and the picture I sent, I got what the number said I wanted.

I called a lady at the company in California who said that she would send a prepaid label to use to send the hammers back and that as soon as she got them, she'd send me a typewriter.

Three weeks later, I called her about the whereabouts of my typewriter. She said it was mailed the week before and that I should have it in two or three more weeks.

Four weeks later, which was five weeks after she mailed it, I called to tell her it hadn't arrived yet. She said she'd send me another one, since the first one must have been lost in the mail. Fine with me.

Within two weeks I had received the second typewriter as well as the first, which had been misdelivered to a neighbor with a similar apartment number who had let it sit on her porch for at least a week before deciding it wasn't going to go away and brought it to me.

Since I knew I was getting a second one, I had lent that one to a friend who then didn't want it because the type wasn't aligned with the ribbon.

I didn't want mine, either, because the capital letters typed above the line, despite the note from a technician in China warranting that he had tested mine and that it was okay.

I called the lady in California and said I was sending both typewriters back and asked her to credit my account for all but the ribbons, which I could use in an old typewriter I have.

She offered to send me another one, but I said I didn't believe I wanted her to do that, but thanks anyway.

I lugged both packages to the post office and sent them off, happy to be shed of the whole business.

Three weeks later I called California to see if the two boxes had arrived and if my account had been credited. The nice man on the other end said yes, the packages were received the week before and that a replacement had just gone out to me.

I gripped the phone and said I'd try the new one, but if I didn't like it, I wanted my account credited.

As soon as it arrived, I took it, unopened, straight to the post office and sent it back.

A year later, heartened by success with ordering books from Amazon.com, I decided to order a dog bed.

Since my dog is a very sweet citizen and I felt that he deserved a really good bed, I placed an order with a reputable mail order company for a neat looking rectangular bed that resembled his old bed except for costing a lot more than his old one did.

My dog and I were very excited when a large but not very heavy box arrived via UPS.

The bed was okay, if a bouncy lifeboat was what a dog wanted to sleep in. Sure, it had a vaguely rectangular shape, but the edges were great big rolls of stuff that enclosed a really small sleeping surface.

I put the bed down for my dog and explained that it was his new bed. I had to coax him into it, since it didn't resemble any bed he'd ever dealt with.

He stepped over into its bouncy sleeping part and stepped right back out. He sat down and looked at it.

I persuaded him to get in it one more time, but he wasn't having any of it. He got right back out and walked out of the room.

I repacked it and took a look at the UPS return label. The note that came with it said that if I used the label, my account credit would be reduced by $5.85. A small price to pay, considering everything.

When I called UPS to arrange a pick-up, the lady said there would be a $10 fee, or I could drive to the nearest UPS store, which was 27 miles away. By my lightning ten-finger calculation, I would be out $15.85 if I did the pick-up option, so I thought not.

She said I could stop any UPS truck I saw and give the package to the driver. Yeah, right.

I shredded the UPS label to avoid identity theft and prepared the box for the U. S. Mail.

On the way to the Post Office, I saw a UPS truck parked in a strip shopping center parking lot. I found the driver and asked him to take the package, which he couldn't do unless it had a UPS label on it.

Seeing as how the required label was shredded, I went to the Post Office and paid $22 to mail the bed back, the cheapest rate they had. The next option was fifty something dollars because of the size of the package.

That's why I don't do mail order.

∞∞

A Walk by the Sea
Patricia Byrd

I'd like to walk by the sea with you

And hold your hand.

We'd talk of things old and new

And the mysteries of God and man.

Namasté
Howatt E. Mallinson

"Namasté!" (A greeting from India) I said to the clerk at

a BP station in Gainesville, GA.

A smile, then eagerly, "Have you been to India?"

"Yes," I answered.

"Where?"

"Agra – the Taj." A big smile.

"And where did you live?" I asked.

"In Hyderabad."

"We visited there, too."

"Where did you stay?" asked the clerk.

"At the Christian Seminary there."

"Oh," smiled the clerk, "my father was a student there for a

year. What did you see in Hyderabad?"

"The museum of the Nizam of Hyderabad. It was fantastic!"

"Yes!" declared the clerk. "My father took me there many

times when I was a boy."

We discussed what we had seen there – the intricately carved

Desk of Napoleon's wife, Josephine; a marble statue of a lovely woman,

but the back part of the statue was the devil Mephistopheles; another

statue of "Veiled Rachel," where the sculptor so skillfully perforated the

marble veil that her face could be seen

through the veil.

"Did you know," I remarked, "that these treasures of the

Nizam are on display now in Atlanta at the High Museum of

Art? My wife and I were there just last week!"

"Oh," exclaimed the clerk, "I didn't know that. I will

try to see them again!"

Perfect strangers when we met, but brothers on separating,

and all because of "Namasté!"

The Water Bottle
Doyle Boyd

I am a water bottle, and I am proud to be a water bottle, proud to exist. I am crystal clear except for the red, white, and blue label which occupies about three inches around my midriff. I hold 25.3 ounces of fat-free and calorie free pure water. My screw-on top is bright blue, and my pop-up cap is a striking red. I can remember the time when I did not exist, and none of my compatriots was in existence. We were just waiting for our time. Long ago, country folks had wells and drew their water up with an elongated metal bucket tied at the end of a rope. Then the water was poured into a water bucket for drinking from a metal dipper. The whole family, and even friends, would dip out of the same bucket and drink out of the same dipper. People wanted to do better, so electric pumps were invented, which led to city water where a whole population could drink from the same source. There were lots of different liquids to drink: beer, wine, carbonated drinks, lemonade, tea, coffee, and Gatorade. Finally, people realized that there was one special liquid, fat-free and calorie free, the healthiest kind of all—water. But humans had grown accustomed to convenience. They could have almost anything—beer or soda at the pop of a can. Eventually, people caught on and discovered water in a bottle, so here I am.

I do not remember where I was made or where I got my first fill of water. It may have been in Little Rock, Arkansas, but I do not recall. Anyhow, I found myself full of the best possible water in a Wal-Mart store in Odessa, Texas. There I was—sitting on the shelf with five of my friends—a six pack. Along came this female citizen with her adult son, who was dressed in western style and pushing a shopping cart. I heard them talking.

"Son, I need some drinking water for my refrigerator."

"Mom, just run some out of your faucet. Let it stand overnight, and tomorrow morning there will be no chlorine odor or taste."

"But I want some spring water," she insisted.

So, he pulled a six pack off the shelf and plunked us into the shopping cart. There I was with my five pals, along with paper towels, a gallon of milk, deodorant, washing machine detergent, a loaf of bread, and a pile of other items.

We went to the check-out station where I got a short joy ride on the conveyor belt. I was scanned over a bright light, and beeped by the cashier who was dressed in a blue Wal-Mart jacket, and plunked into the bottom of the gray shopping cart. Soon, lots of plastic bags full of other things were dropped all around me. The cart started rolling and bumping on irregularities in the floor, and soon the cool temperature began to get warmer. All I could see were cars and trucks, legs and Bermuda shorts, sneakers and sandals, and lamp posts.

Next thing I knew, I was loaded into the back of a full-sized, white pickup truck with a dual cab. As we departed the parking lot, I could feel a warm breeze blowing on my cap. In about fifteen minutes, we stopped in the driveway of a yellow brick house. My group was taken into the residence and placed on the kitchen counter. I was chosen for the refrigerator duty so quickly that I had no time for goodbyes to my pals. I was looking around at a jug of milk, some sodas, and storage containers when the light went out and it was total blackness. Occasionally, the light would come on, and then go out. This was followed by a longer period of darkness. It must have been the next morning when the door was opened and the lady grabbed me by the middle, broke the seal, popped up the top, and began draining my spring water—a sip at a time. This went on all through the day until finally I was empty.

Here I go to the recycle bin where I will eventually be crushed, I thought. However, my cap was removed, and I found myself under the kitchen faucet being refilled with chlorinated water. Yuk! But I was pleased because I liked the refrigerator with its colors and nice cool temperature all the time. The next thing I knew, I was lying on my back in a chest-type box, which turned out to be a deep freeze. Gee, it got colder and colder, and it was lights out for days at a time.

Early one morning I was lying on my back meditating when the lid opened and I heard a lady say, "Here is a bottle of ice that you can put into your cooler to keep your drinks and snacks cool during your trip."

I thought, What is this? I am going on a trip, and I am not yet retired?

I heard some talk about how one gets on I-20 going east, and then the cooler was closed. I wished that I knew when there would be daylight and darkness, and where we were going.

I wanted to stay in Odessa since I had heard George Bush lived there; I had heard, however, that after Odessa, he and his family moved to Midland, Texas where the richer Texans lived. That was only about twenty-five miles east on I-20. Odessa had some history according to the lady in the front seat. It seems that Odessa originated from the Russian Odessa on the Black Sea. Someone opened the cooler in Midland, and I got a peek at the affluent city. I noticed a number of skyscrapers which shot upwards from the flat Texas terrain. Then the cooler was closed again.

Somewhere east of Big Spring, Texas, the cooler was opened again and the lady said, "Let's use the rest room first, then we will have something to drink."

I was beginning to thaw out and my ice was becoming liquid. Pop, the cooler closed.

Shortly, the cooler opened again and a man noticed my water and said, "This is what I need." So he drank all of the melted water and left only the ice.

The trip became uneventful until the cooler opened and I heard some talk about which exit to take in Arlington. We made it to the two-story house in a residential area, and since I was almost empty, I was returned to the cooler.

The next day I was refilled with water and was taken outside to see the sights. I saw four adults concentrating on building a small shop out of lumber while two girls jumped on a nearby trampoline. Because of hot weather, I was emptied and refilled several times during the day.

After several days, I was back in the cooler and headed east. Most of my time was spent in the cooler, but one day I sat in the bottle holder in the console, between the two front seats. I could see in the rear view mirror, a woman on my left and a man on my right. Sometimes I could see the tops of buildings on the right and the left. There were white clouds, blue skies, and once, a plane almost beyond sight. My view was blocked once while the man looked at a roadmap that he had unfolded. Suddenly, I heard him say that we were approaching Tyler, Texas. He folded away the map and began reading out of <u>A Roadside History of Texas,</u> by Leon C. Mertz. We all learned that President John Tyler was responsible for the name of this town. And the man said so many Indians were killed here that it ended the Cherokee-Texas War. He shared that over 6,000 Union troops were once held near Tyler in Camp Ford, and at one time the rose industry made Tyler famous, as one-half of all rose bushes were grown within a ten mile radius of Tyler. After that lesson, it was back to the cooler for me.

I was in and out of the cooler, but out enough to learn that we zoomed through the rest of Texas, then Louisiana, Mississippi, Alabama, and finally arrived in Florida where I saw "granny" and several of her descendants. There the man filled me with some refreshing well water straight out of a faucet. After a short stay, we left early one morning and arrived later that day in Milledgeville, Georgia.

This man seemed to be attached to me. He even took me with him to his work on a "Habitat House." He would work and sip—and refill. I heard him tell someone that he used me to ensure that he drank adequate water each day.

The advantage for me is that I get lots of attention.

The Crack of Dawn*

Susan Lindsley

I heard the crack of dawn and knew that's why I came awake,
For every dawn I hear the sound of day about to break

And every day I rush about, afraid that night will fall
And crumble into pieces that can not be fixed at all.

So like a broken egg the night could spill out every where
And mingle with the broken dawn till both are lost somewhere.

*In memory of my aunt Susan Myrick,
who could never bear to see the day break.*

Catch of the Day
Jan Williams

For Christmas one year my husband, Bob, had requested a fly-fishing rod and reel. Not that he knew how to fly fish, but he wanted to learn the "art" of fly fishing. After all, he had fished all of his life, so what's so hard about fly fishing?

Being the dutiful wife I was, I bought him a fly-fishing set with the stipulation that, if he was not pleased, he could return it—no questions asked. Well, when he opened his present on Christmas morning, his eyes lighted up like a Christmas tree. He was as excited as any of the kids! He could hardly wait for the crowd to clear out so he could go fishing. Soon after lunch he saw his chance to get away.

Donning his best fishing clothes—tattered jacket, old blue jeans and crumpled hat—off he went to the lake that was within walking distance of the house. I got a good book and settled down for a nice quiet afternoon of reading. About 30 minutes into this nice quiet time I heard the backdoor open and Bob shouting for me to come look! Of course, I thought it was the "catch of the day" and we would be having fish for dinner. When I got to the kitchen I saw Bob standing in the middle of the room with this bright yellow fishing lure caught in the middle of his upper lip. He was jabbering something about me getting the wire cutters and cutting this hook off so that I could pull-l-l-l this lure out of his upper lip. While he was talking, the feathers were tickling his nose and he kept slapping at the feathers while trying to convince me that all I needed to do was to get the wire cutters and snip off the hook! Well, I was in hysterics (not from fright, but from laughter). That was the funniest sight I had ever seen! I was trying to keep some composure about this matter, but I found it hard to do. He kept saying these feathers were tickling his nose. I told him if he would stop breathing I thought that would solve the problem (that was NOT received well); I told him I would NOT cut off the hook, but I would take him to the emergency room at the hospital, and they could cut it off for him. Reluctantly he agreed, so we loaded up in the car and off we sped to the local hospital (on Christmas Day)! As we were barreling down I-75, cars began to pass us, honk the horn, laugh and point at Bob. Did I mention he was still talking and swatting at the yellow feathers that were tickling his nose? We finally arrived at the emergency room. I drove up to the door and asked him to get out and get in line; I would be there as soon as I parked the car. I needed one more guffaw before I faced the medical staff.

When I entered the emergency room Bob was nowhere to be found. Finally, I asked the nurse and she grinned and said, "I took him back to the admissions desk." I saw him sitting there while the clerk was asking questions. I opened the door and heard her ask his name, address, etc.

"What seems to be your problem?" (Up to that point she had not bothered to look at him.)

He said, "Well, I have this fishing lure in my upper lip."

With that she whirled around, took one look at him and went running out the door, trying hard not to laugh in his face. Immediately, she returned and said, "The doctor will see you now."

We were taken to one of those "holding" rooms to wait for the doctor. Soon we heard him outside the door—reading the chart— laughing heartily, and, upon opening the door and seeing Bob with the yellow feathers wiggling as he talked, he said, "Well, Buddy, that is one that didn't get away!"

&)CR

Snazzy Sunday
Shane Riner

Lying on a Sunday
All bright
A strange new day
With no memory intact
Of the next bill to pay
To lie in the heat,
As if the last days of summer
Had just begun
My intention is not
to fake my job,
Nor anything else,
but today is a Sunday,
And today will be
My day!

Cherry Blossom Festival
Evangeline Lundy

Every spring in Macon you will hear the phrase "think pink" many times. The Cherry Blossom Festival evolved over many years. It began as a simple idea of "keeping Macon clean and beautiful."

Carolyn Crayton worked with that idea and with Mr. William Fickling's passion for the Japanese Yoshino cherry trees. Today, thanks to their efforts, it has developed into an international event. It ranks among the top of the festivals in the USA and has a huge economical impact on Macon and surrounding areas.

Pink—when the word is heard, it brings to mind many different images—vibrant   warm pink, hot pink, and deep, rich fuchsia pink. But the color of the Yoshino cherry blossom is a shade of "barely pink." It is said that Macon has more cherry trees than any other city in the world. It is easy to believe if you are walking among the trees and a strong breeze causes the tree limbs to move. The delicate petals fall on your head and into your hair. They caress your cheeks as they float downward. They pass by your eyelashes like a butterfly kiss, as they fall imperceptibly onto your shoulders. At certain times of the day in some of the parks—usually in late afternoon, the boughs are silhouetted against the sky in a free-form outline that catches your attention with the stark beauty of the scene.

When the dates of the festival approach, there is much anxiety over whether or not the blooms will appear at the scheduled time. Sometimes nature does not cooperate and they do not bloom when expected. However, I remember one year when they bloomed profusely at the appropriate time, and so did everything else. It seemed that nature conspired to make each and every one of the carefully planted and nurtured plants to bloom at the same time, at the height of the blooming of the cherry blossom trees. That year was the only one I can remember when that happened. Beauty surrounded us—at our feet, over our heads, into the azure sky, frosted with huge, puffy light blue and white clouds. It seemed to me that our good Lord had decided to give us a rare gift—one we could cherish forever.

Every Morning Mercies New
Ethelene Dyer Jones

It is of the Lord's mercies that we are not consumed, because His compassions fail not. They are new every morning; great is Thy faithfulness.
—Lamentations 3:22-23.

Oh! The delight of morning
When birds are on the wing;
When squirrels scamper for food
And Nature wakes to sing!

Another day to embrace life,
To rejoice with exultant thanks;
To know that whatever happens
God keeps us in His ranks!

What beauty for our eyes to see,
What joy within our hearts
When Spring in all its splendor
With bursting new growth starts!

At times in Winter we wonder
Will darkness and nighttime cease;
But on a bright Spring morning
Joy floods with amazing peace.

As duties call and crowd me,
May this Spring morning etch its place
Of reassurance on this journey
That God walks with me in life's race.

Mom
Irwin Gates

When I was a little shaver in Los Angeles, 1940, I used to spend my time at home with my mother. I never thought of my mother in descriptive words: five-foot-four inches tall, with long black hair interspersed with threads of grey, which she combed one hundred strokes every night and wore in two buns. She had distinctive, symmetrical features clothed with a gently smooth skin. I always thought of her by what she did. She cooked all the meals, sewed a little, darned socks, replaced buttons, washed and hung out clothes to dry on the line, ironed and placed clothes in the drawers where they would be when it was time to wear them. She carefully planted her dahlias and gladiolus, weeded the garden which was composted with leaves and fertilized in a well laid out plan, which left enough grass to allow a cleaning underneath the clothesline. She frequently watered the ferns, which grew on the north side of the house. The house was swept, vacuumed, and dusted regularly. I always thought of her this way, because this WAS living for her.

I have what my eye doctor called a lazy left eye. He had me wear glasses with a patch over my right eye so that I would be forced to use my left eye. He also had me come to his office for eye exercises. His office was located downtown. My mother took me for these appointments.

"We have to leave early today. I want to pick up a couple of things at Bullocks Department Store."

When we left home on Harvard Boulevard, we walked north to Third Street where we turned right for a block to wait for the streetcar.

"Watch for an R or S."

"Okay, take my hand."

We stepped out into the passenger island to signal to conductor that we wanted to board.

"At least we didn't get the R car, which would require a transfer."

The streetcar was like a downsized train, which ran on steel tacks with steel wheels. The bottom of the vehicle was painted yellow, and the top rust colored. Windows around the area where passengers sat allowed them to view the passing parade as they traveled. Lights were in the middle of the front and back. On top were fishing pole-like devises, which attached to an overhead power line. Rectangular windows on the roof allowed light to come in. As I stepped onboard, I could see a tower box with glass sides and a trapdoor which allowed the conductor to count the change when we put it in the box.

"Three tokens, please."

The conductor took her dime and handed her the tokens. She dropped two in the box.

"Mom, may I sit by the window?"

The seats on the streetcar were wood with a pivot on then that allowed them to be swung from a tilt to the back to a tilt to the front. When the car reached the end of the line, the conductor would go through and set the seats so that they would be tilted in the opposite direction. He would carry his throttle handle and change box to the new front for the return trip. Outside he would change the power pole so that it slanted to the back for the new direction.

"Mom, may I pull the cord to ring the bell?"

"I'll let you know when."

People were walking up and down both sides of the street. Some were in a hurry. Others seemed to be taking in the displays in the department store windows. They seemed to be imagining how the particular products would look in their homes.

"You may pull the cord now."

We made our way from the streetcar to Bullocks.

"May I go to the toy department?"

"Not right now."

We stepped up to some sliding doors and pushed a button. The hand above the doors pointed to a five. The hand started down: 4, 3, 2, 1. The doors opened and people started pouring out. Soon they were out and we entered. My stomach sank as the elevator went up. When the elevator stopped, my stomach returned to normal. We went to the clothing department, then to the ladies section, where she looked for gloves in her size, 7. She found a black pair that fitted her perfectly.

"Please put these on my Bullocks charge plate."

The clerk put the imprinted sales slip in a canister, which was shot by air through a tube to the credit department. Ten minutes later the canister was back and the transaction was complete.

"Thank you for shopping Bullocks."

We took the escalator down one flight to the appliance department. She looked over the toasters and decided to buy a Toastmaster.

"Please have the toaster shipped to our home."

"Is the address the same as on you charge plate?"

"Yes, it is."

"We'll be happy to have it sent by one of our delivery trucks. Thank you for shopping with Bullocks."

"Can we go to the toy department now?"

"Yes, we can go now."

The toy department, located on the second floor, was my favorite place in the whole store. With sparkling eyes, I looked at the wagons, bikes, scooters and other toys. The toy department had a hardwood slide which paralleled an inclined floor to the mezzanine. I slid down the slide and mother took the incline.

"We have to move along now so we won't be late for your appointment."

Walking along the sidewalk, my mother's German/French heritage came out.

"Pull you shoulders back. Walk beside me."

In a nearby building we took a high-speed elevator to the seventh floor, which left my stomach with that sinking feeling again. We went down the hall and turned to the right to Dr. Clarence Wright's office. We informed the receptionist of our presence. Five minutes later she called me in.

"Master Gates, you may come in now."

I went into a black cubicle.

"Put your chin in the cup. Follow the movement of the red light. I'll be back in a few minutes."

My right eye was covered, while my left eye watched a red light move around in different patterns. Then the color was changed to green and the process repeated. Dr. Wright spoke to my mother in my presence, "Mrs. Gates, have Irwin continue to wear a patch over his right eye for thirty minutes each day."

The receptionist made another appointment for me. The elevator dropped us to the ground floor and we made our way to the streetcar stop. As we left the downtown area on the streetcar, the high buildings gave way to shorter ones. The number of people on the street decreased with the lowering of the building heights. One-story buildings lined the business street on which we traveled. As we rounded the corner, the arm came off the overhead power line. The conductor had to get out of the streetcar and reset the power arm back onto the power line so that we could continue on our journey.

"Look Mom, there's Bimini Baths."

I imagined myself going to Bimini Baths, which has series of heated pools on the inside and a cold-water pool on the outside. My friends and I would play tag and show off by splashing into the water from the diving board. We would make cannonballs, flips, and nonsense dives from the board.

"You may go there with your friends when you're out of school."

"Why are people so different?"

"What do you mean?"

"Some are tall, others short; some thin, others fat; some fast, others slow. They have different colors of skin: white, yellow, brown and black."

"The differences give us variety. You wouldn't want everyone to look the same."

"I guess not, it wouldn't be much fun watching them."

The trip home passed rapidly. Before we knew it, we were walking to our home. As we stepped in, it felt good to be back.

ℰ⅃ℭℜ

Crystal clear water
Cool and sparkling in the glass,
Satisfies my thirst.

*****

The murky old pond;
A fish jumps into the air,
The splash of water.
                                     -M.T. Knight

The Bottle Tree
Mary Purcell

Previously published:
Mary B. Purcell, "The Bottle Tree," O, Georgia!, ed. Terri Pepper Gavulic (Cummings: Humpus Bumpus Press, 2000) 219-223.

Jimmy awakened as his wife's left hand caught him square on the face. "Damn it, woman! What's wrong with you?" he asked, more to himself than to Annie Mae. He'd seen her like this before—fightin' that devil inside her head. Despite the wet and cold January night, sweat beaded on her forehead. Turning back and forth and kicking away the covers, she moaned as she tossed her hands from side to side. She'd start to shakin' soon. Then, she'd come full awake—scream some kind of crazy stuff about that red bottle, and push him out of their warm bed into the cold night.

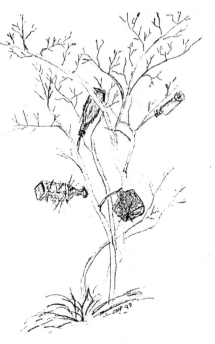

Jimmy squirmed around in the bed waiting for her eyes to open. They did! "Go get it!" she demanded. Jimmy mumbled to himself as he climbed out of bed.

"The red one. Get the red one. He's kicked himself off that bottle tree again. I know it. Lord, what a devil's inside that thing! Hurry up, Jimmy. Lord, you is slow!"

Jimmy pulled on his boots and wrapped a coat around his nakedness. He'd take enough time for that.

The door banged shut, covering the sound of Jimmy cursing B&W, Annie Mae's old dog, curled up sound asleep next to the fireplace. He stumbled off the porch and down the three steps into the yard. Besides being cold, the night was a solid sheet of black. "Gonna' picks me up a snake out here one of these nights," Jimmy whispered. "Then she'll be sorry she sent me out here like this."

He worked his way around the well and stepped silently into the small grove of crepe myrtle. He walked to the bottle tree and leaned over, feeling with his hands for any bottle on the ground and gibbering to himself. "Ain't never seen such as this," he groaned, as his fingers fastened onto the familiar smooth feel of glass. He picked up the bottle, placing his thumb over the smooth curved top. "Ain't no used taking no chances," he muttered. He didn't even try to see if it was the right color. He knew it was the red one—always was!

Jimmy stomped back up the stairs, opened the door with his free hand, and walked in. Annie Mae was full awake and pacing the floor. "Hand it here!" she demanded. "If'n I had a switch I could reach into that bottle, I'd tan his hide! He just loves upsetting me like this."

Jimmy offered her the bottle—his thumb still over the curved top. The light of the fire in the fireplace sparkled through the red bottle as Annie Mae and Jimmy exchanged possession. She slipped her thumb over the opening as Jimmy let his fall away.

"Can we go back to sleep now?" Jimmy asked, knowing there would be no more real sleep.

Annie Mae didn't feel a need to answer. She just took the bottle and held it up to the firelight.

B&W came full awake, barking at Annie Mae and her red bottle. "Shut your mouth, you mutt!" Jimmy hollered. "Slept through all the good stuff. Why, if I was a robber, you'd have let me come right on in and—"

"Leave him alone, Jimmy," Annie Mae screamed. "This here haint is bad enough without you and B&W making it worser!"

Annie Mae held the bottle up to her eyes, rolling it from side to side to catch each shaft of firelight as it danced through the glass. "I can't keep you inside," she said. "I try and try—but you kick off the bottle tree the minute my back is turned. What am I going to do? I knows and you knows that this ain't funny. I needs my sleep—and you wants your freedom. Jimmy, give me that cork over there out of the bottom of that old salt shaker. I think it'll hold him 'till morning. I don't want him wanderin' around in here. He'll make some kind of mischief before mornin' if'n I let him stay out."

Jimmy popped the cork out of the bottom of the salt shaker and handed it to Annie Mae. She plugged the hole and set herself down in the old rocker beside the rag pile where B&W slept. "I'll rock him to sleep," she said. "That's what it takes."

"How long you gonna be, Annie Mae?"

"Might be all night. You go on to bed."

Jimmy shook his head as he watched Annie Mae rocking. Slowly, he walked into the darkened bedroom. Annie Mae heard the boots hit the floor, but she was too busy singing to say good night. She began to hum and her humming became a lullaby. "You go to sleep now," she coaxed. "No use you trying to fight it. What kind of trouble have you been in tonight?" she asked the red bottle. "It's always something. You worser than a mean dog!"

B&W began barking and jumping around wildly. "I ain't talkin' about you, B&W. I be talking about this here haint. He done caused me more trouble than I can gets myself out of. He always does, when he sets to kicking his mean carcass off'n that tree. I try to keeps him happy, but he hunts the mischief. Once he got out and it was two days before I catch him and put him back on that bottle tree. Know what he does? He gets my Jimmy real drunk, and the law done put him in jail. Cost me $25 to get his sorry ass back. I had to go down there and beg them to take my money. Well, I looked and found this here red bottle off the tree. I puts it back and things get better. Annie Mae don't need no train to run over her brain to make the right connections. Her connections is just fine.

"Take that salesman what stopped off here with one of those rolling stores, trying to sell me a pot mender. I told him, 'I don't need no pot mender,' but he keeps on insisting. I said that my pots don't need no mending, so he says for me to show him. I ain't never seen afore or after like him. He just barges inside the house, goes to the pot shelf behind the cook stove and commences to pull down all three of my pots. He looks them over real good, then he says, 'You right. You don't need no pot mender. You need me!'

"Before I know what is going on, he is all over me. Lord a mercy! I can't breathe or nothin'. He's mended more than pots with them hands 'cause they can—Lord, whew! I scream for Jimmy—he ain't no where round. I know my bottle is off the tree for sure! I says, 'Let me go, you fool. I got to find my bottle.' Well, the salesman must think I mean my drinking stuff, so he turns me loose. I runs for the door and out into the yard—straight to that damn tree. Sure enough, that red bottle is a layin' right there on the ground underneath that tree. Jimmy walks up about the time I picks up the bottle and puts it back on the tree. The salesman sees Jimmy and slips out the back door. I see him running like hell out the garden way. Then, he sneaks around to the front, walks up to my Jimmy and don't even look my way while he talks to him about buying some liniment for his joints. I go round them and in the house. I ain't never seen him again. But Julia Bailey says she seen him, and he can mend her pots anytime he be in town."

Annie Mae continued to rock, holding the red bottle like it was a baby, nestled against her large bosom. "I know what it's like—being kept bottled up. Can't go nowhere or do nothing lessin' it pleases someone else. But baby, you is a troublemaker. Go to sleep now. Hush. Hush."

Jimmy found her and the bottle in that very same position come morning. He leaned over and kissed Annie Mae, holding the precious bottle against her chest so that it would not fall. "Lord a mercy," Annie Mae groaned. "Is it morning?" Jimmy didn't answer; he just motioned for her to get up.

"Come on, let's put the bottle back on the tree," he said, "time to get to work." Jimmy was dressed, but Annie Mae still had on one of his old work shirts she used as a nightgown, as they moved into the yard to put the bottle back on the tree.

"I don't know why you keep on doing this," Jimmy said. "He'll just get loose again, and you'll have another bad night."

"You know why, Jimmy. I can't let him get away. You know how much trouble he can cause. You remember that time the law—"

"Don't start that again," Jimmy pleaded.

"Well, you know how it can get."

Annie Mae pushed the cork inside the narrow neck of the red bottle just as she and Jimmy reached the crepe myrtle tree. She kept her thumb over the opening until she found the right branch, then she slipped the bottle's narrow neck onto the slim branch.

"Now," she said, "you behave yourself—if'n you can."

Mrs. Ross, Annie Mae's new boss, drove up the driveway about the time the bottle slid in place. "Oh hell," Annie Mae mumbled, "I'll catch it now; I'm late for work."

As she ran for the porch, Mrs. Ross opened the door of her shiny Plymouth and glided out the driver's side. Pointing to the bottle tree, she asked Annie Mae to explain what it was. "I've never noticed it before," she stated, as she walked toward the bottles sparkling in the early morning light and beckoned Annie Mae to join her.

"It's just an old bottle tree, Mrs. Ross," Annie Mae answered, walking in her direction, drawing the old work shirt close to her body.

"What's the significance of the tree? It must mean something."

"This be just an old crepe myrtle. I puts the bottles all over the tree—the browns, whites, yellows, greens, blues, and the red one. They are to catch haints, Mrs. Ross.

122

"I use my bottles to catch evil spirits; keeps them out of my house and away from me and my Jimmy. They get real curious. And they like glass, Mrs. Ross. See how the sun makes sparkles in the bottles," Annie Mae said, as she pointed to the different colored bottles on the tree. "Well, the haints, I mean the spirits, can climb in, enjoy the sun and the sparkle light. They grow fat and lazy, then they can't get out of the skinny neck of the bottle anymore. They be trapped. Can't cause Annie Mae and Jimmy no trouble."

Mrs. Ross laughed. "You believe that stuff, Annie Mae?"

"Don't you, Mrs. Ross?" Annie Mae looked at her sparkling bottles and touched the glass, holding the colors in her hand and heart.

"Hurry, if you would, Annie Mae. I'm a little early because we've a mess to clean up this morning. A water pipe broke under the kitchen sink last night, and I have two inches of water everywhere."

Annie Mae tapped the red bottle with her index finger—"You devil," she said under her breath. "I'll be just a minute, Mrs. Ross. Let me put some clothes on these bones."

ᔓᙆ

The lone butterfly

Never appears in a hurry,

Even when pursued.

I kept it a secret

The first dream of the year,

And smiled to myself.

                                    -M.T. Knight

The Red Maple Christmas
Doyle Boyd

The spindly red maple
Had been damaged
Over the Years…surrounded
By dominant trees bigger
Around and much taller.

The pines could be
Used for pulpwood or
Timber; They could
Make paper or a
Building to remember.

Oaks grew much
Larger and made the
Squirrels a thoroughfare
And acorn meals
For the winter.

Dogwoods showed off in the spring
With sheets of white flowers.
And people who looked
In awe commented about
The beauty of spring.

Then, there were the spider lilies;
They took their turns…
The tips of their spikes
Blossomed with tentacles that
Appeared hot enough to burn.

There was nothing to remember
About a crippled maple
But its smooth, white bark.
Yet, in the middle of November,
The maple took heart with a plan.

It would color its leaves and
Bring excitement to man. So the
Leaves were painted a bright red.
And on the same leaves would be
Equally intense yellow,

So that anyone walking
Under the tree would
See the fallen but
Powerfully colored leaves
And pick up one and marvel.

How well the red maple had
Decorated the forest! From under
This tree one could see the fresh fallen
Tan needles of the pine and the
Colorless dark brown leaves of the oaks.

And at this point, the maple
Decided to use its bright colors
To announce the coming of an
Event to remember, which would
Occur on the twenty-fifth of December.

ॐ

Trees stronger than steel,

Reach upward toward the sky

Such gentle giants.
                              -M.T. Knight

Whatever Happened to the True Meaning of Christmas?
Sandy Jasnau

Over two thousand years ago, God sent us the wondrous gift of Jesus Christ to teach us all why we are here in this world. Christ brought us many wonderful gifts such as love, kindness, patience, faith in God, and knowledge of God.

He also taught us not to criticize each other or to kill our fellow man, as each one of us is part of God's creation. Although many of us have developed these attributes of God, others have a good bit of work to do in developing these spiritual qualities. Our world is in turmoil because religions have strayed far from the original teachings of their Prophets.

Upon becoming a member of the Baha'i Faith, I learned that all the major religions have come from the same God, teaching us to love one another; to do unto others as we would have them do unto us (the Golden Rule); and promising, if we follow theses teachings, our world will unite in peace. Christians all repeat in the Lord's Prayer, "Thy Kingdom come, Thy will be done on earth as it is in Heaven." Does it make any sense to fight and kill each other because we think OUR faith is the only way to God?

Peace begins in the heart of each one of us, and, to develop this, we must all learn to respect and care for everyone regardless of race, religion, or ethnic background...because we are all created by the same Father.

Isn't this what Christmas should be about?

The Lost Bedtime Story

Shane Riner

For those who are lost
For those who will never be found
To be put into the world
And tossed around
For all the sorrow
At every passing minute
For all that flutters within you
For the last note
To the tear that silenced you
Reaching for the breath
The one that you
Couldn't have wished for
For all that you've forgotten
For the piano that you could never play
For the last cry you have wept
At the angel's touch you shall always
Reach for
At the arm of the trust
At the lover's note
The mud on the grass where you fell
All the signs you missed
Coming back from hell
For just to wonder
The force that made the story straight
For all you have
You have me

The Voice Inside My Head

Martha J. Williams

"The life I touch for good or ill will touch another life, and in turn another, until who knows where the trembling stops or in what far place my touch will be felt.

-Frederick Buechner

There have been times during my life
When I would look up to the sky and say,
"Lord, stop the World;
I want to get off today."

Then the voice in my head would reply, "NO, not yet.
You still have a job to do.
My plans for you have been set.
If you stop now, you will have regrets."

"Lord, stop the World; I want to get off today."
Again the voice inside my head will say,
"NO, not today – no way;
Try to see things my way."

This voice in my head keeps telling me,
To love all the people that I meet.
"Help them to understand that my kingdom
Is what they must seek."

The voice tells me to love my fellow man,
Help them to understand, that they all
Have a life that is planned.
It is up to me to lend them a helping hand.

"Lord, what part do I play in your divine plan?
Please help me; I am trying to understand.
Do I have what it takes to help my fellow man?
Or do I wait until you reveal your entire plan?"

"Lord, stop the World; I want to get off today."
Again, the voice would say, "NO, not today,
There are hundreds of children who need you.
No one touches their hearts as you do."

"I am getting tired, Lord.
Sometimes I feel that my work is in vain.
My heart is so full of pain!
Please help me before I go insane."

"Look up, my child," the voice would say.
"Just take small steps, one, two, three, four a day.
I will continue to show you the way.
Just continue to pray.
Tomorrow will be a better day."

෨෬

Ice Cream

Patricia S. Byrd

I used to walk down a country road

Slowly licking a treasured ice cream cone,

Trying my best to make it last

Until we reached home.

Emergency
Harriett Davis

Yesterday, I was having an uneventful day. I was just fooling around in my kitchen, when suddenly, disaster struck. The unthinkable happened. I had to tell someone. I called Natalie, my best friend and confidant. She's the best friend I ever had because she understands me.

I called Natalie's cell phone. Her voice mail picked up. I called her car phone, there was no answer. I beeped her, no response. I faxed and e-mailed her, no reply. This was unreal. I beeped her again and put in 911; she'd know it was an emergency and call me right back. But there was still no response. And I thought to myself, Natalie's lack of response is getting on my nerves.

Beginning to lose my patience, I dialed Natalie again. A recording stated, "Your party is not accepting calls at this time." What was that supposed to mean? Not a quitter, I dialed again. I breathed a sigh of relief when Natalie said, "Hello." Quickly I yelled, "Girl, I have an emergency over here." But her voice continued, "We are not home right now. If you have a message for Natalie, press 1; for Nathan, Sr., press 2; Junior, press 3; Neandra, press 4; Rover, press 5; Kitty Kat, press 6." My nerves were on edge. I pressed 1 and yelled, "It's an emer…" The tape ended. I took a deep breath and counted to ten, trying hard not to say any bad words. After composing myself, I dialed back, pressed 1 and yelled, "Emergency, call me."

Patiently I waited, and I waited, for two whole minutes, then I dialed again. This time a strange voice said, "I star 69 you. You had the right number, only your timing is off. If I catch you fooling around with my husband, I'm going to kick your _ _ _."

Expeditiously, I hung up. But if I had known her name or number, I would have called her back and told her a thing or two.

Then it dawned on me. What if something has happened to Natalie and her family? I began to worry. I was frantic. I had to do something. Desperate, I got in my car and drove across town to the Piggly Wiggly. I couldn't think of anything else to do, so I sent Natalie a telegram. It stated, "Call me immediately/It's an emergency."

On the way home, I started thinking how selfish I was. Here I was worried about my problems, when Natalie and her family were somewhere possibly fighting for their very lives. Distraught, I cried all the way home. But as I drove into my driveway, I noticed someone knocking on my door. I was in no mood for company. I was in mourning for the best friend I ever had.

But it was Natalie. "**Natalie**," I screamed, jumping out of the car. "Girl, I'm so happy to see you; I've been worried sick. I thought something had happened to you. Thank God, you're safe," I cried.

Natalie looked at me, hands on her hips. She didn't care about my tears. Natalie just looked at me and said, "If I've told you once, I've told you a thousand times, I am not impressed by your theatrics, and I don't appreciate all this drama. You are a drama queen."

And at that moment I thought, "She makes me sick. I can't stand her...Miss High and Mighty."

Natalie continued, "If you wanted me so badly, why didn't you just walk across the street to my house...and barge in without knocking like you usually do?"

I'd never even thought about that.

"You were just over to my house two hours ago. What's so all fired important? What's the emergency?"

I looked my dearest friend in the eye, and I said, "I, um, was ah, baking...and I ran out of sugar...girl friend, you got any?"

ℰ✺ℭℛ

Large puffy white clouds

Floating along in the air,

Like cotton candy.
                        -M.T. Knight

A Royal Life
Marie Horton and Carrie Cox

My story begins in Paris in the mid 1800s. I have good reason to believe I am of a royal line, because the label burned into my inner body is that of a very famous violin hand-crafter. While of a later vintage than the Stradivarius, Amati and the few well-known earlier craftsmen, Vuillaume was certainly a name to be reckoned with. Unfortunately, my roots are cloudy because copiers were known to sometimes insert famous and false labeling into their nearly perfect imitations, leaving some of us between real class or good copy. Only extensive and expensive research can really assess my value. No family is left to provide answers.

It is known that my first purchaser was a wealthy and discerning woman who had difficulty with lessons, lost her first intense interest to play and gave me to a favorite nephew who was about nine or ten years old at the time. Bill loved music, but his real skills were in other things, so I still had not found my rightful destiny.

But Bill finally married Annie Laurie who played many instruments and she certainly mastered my strings—finally transforming me into a fiddle! Do not laugh; good fiddlers were almost as rare as the instruments they played. You see, violins were not turned out *en masse*; they were expensive and found in homes where classical music was favored.

However, music was evolving away from Lohengrin, Brahms, Bach, Beethoven and such. The "Doughboys" had at last returned from World War I, and everyone was seeking a change of mood. As usual, music would provide the leavening. Tin Pan Alley was busy, and you were likely to hear songs of the "Roaring Twenties," "The Charleston," "Alexander's Ragtime Band" or "Dark Town Strutter's Ball."

Bill formed a family band which included his children. With them and Annie's direction, I became a stellar attraction; well known throughout Central Georgia in the crucial years of the Second World War —and the demands were great. Everyone was hungry for a few carefree hours of freedom from war losses and/or other worries, depressions, deprivations, etc. The whole nation was an intensive care unit.

Locally, I was a success at school functions of every kind, high school or elementary class plays, teacher's group, proms and wherever music was required. Saturday afternoons could often find me at the Boys Training School, a center for wayward youth—no criminals among them. We also entertained prisoners who had been sent here from other state institutions to help rebuild the Old State Capital after it had burned.

These performances were at the request of state wardens and the men were very courteous and well behaved.

Annie entered a fiddlers contest at the local Campus Theatre, and despite strong competition, she made me winner of the first place prize. We played on stage in Atlanta with the Cross-Roads Follies, a collection of single or group entertainers of many talents, all well known and loved. WE were applauded heartily and invited to return at any time.

Of course we were involved in worship services at many places, for varied denominations, and we were the only music provided for a group of residents on the north side of town. They were meeting in the old Georgia Railroad Depot and holding Sunday school classes in the trolley car; this church grew into its present long standing status as a leader among local churches.

Oh, I have memories.

My last musicals were very private. The son of the family was diagnosed with a terminal illness. During the long months of waiting, he wanted Annie to play while he accompanied her on his guitar and sang hymns. His last request and my last performance was the beloved plea, "Just As I Am."

I have run the gamut. Born for classical music, graduating into a lighter vein of Tin Pan Alley, popular music, country and western music and lastly to bring comfort through hymns to a family during the final days of their loved one.

For years now a spectator only, I rest on a wall, where from a glass-enclosed shadow box I see my family of today—a generation no longer in touch with my world, nor am I with theirs. But hope remains as I remember an old story about an aged and rather rare violin on display at a prominent auction house. Patrons looked without interest until an elderly gentleman picked the instrument up, put it tenderly under the chin and played a haunting rhapsody from the long-silent strings. Furious bidding ensued and the violin brought a highly satisfactory sum into the auction total. All because of a Master's touch—the musician was later identified as Jascha Heifitz of international renown as a violinist and composer.

So who knows? For now—I just wait.

Remembering Moore's Forge Bridge
Geloria Phelps

A recent article in a local newspaper entitled "FBI Files Shed New Light on Lynching" brought back a flood of childhood memories for me. This incident involved the lynching of two black couples at Moore's Ford Bridge on the Appalachee River in Walton County, Georgia, in 1946.

I was six years old at the time, living on a farm in Barrow County with my parents and five other siblings. Barrow County joins Walton County at the Appalachee River. Both Barrow and Walton Counties were rural farming communities in Northeast Georgia. Some Blacks owned their own farms, but many were sharecroppers and lived on farms owned by while landlords. At one time my family lived in Walton County. They were sharecroppers until my father purchased a farm in Barrow County, and the family moved there. I was the first child in the family to be born in Barrow County.

I cannot say that I actually remember this event, but my recollections stem from hearing my family and others in the community recount the story. One particular event that stands out in my mind was recounted by my mother. She told about the day my father returned home from doing his weekly shopping in Monroe on a Saturday afternoon and told her that his cousin's son, who was nineteen years old at the time, had been beaten badly by some unidentified white men, and he was not expected to live. This beating was the result of his having testified to the FBI agents investigating the case that prior to the lynching he had seen some white men cleaning their guns, sharpening knives, and tying nooses at the livery stable near the ice house where he worked.

Fear gripped the community and paid a visit to our house that night. My mother said she was so afraid that she put out all the lamps in the house. She placed quilts on the floor around the heater in the sitting room and we all slept together on the floor. My mother said she had never experienced that type of fear in her life, and the feeling of helplessness was hard to describe.

Fear also visited the home of my first cousin who actually lived in the Moore's Ford Bridge Community. My cousin had just given birth to a baby girl. Her family was so frightened that they held up in the house and did not venture outside the house for many days. As a result of this, the baby contracted pneumonia and almost died.

My aunt, who also lived near the lynching site, recalled that the two couples had purchased groceries at one of the local grocery stores in Monroe before they were taken to the lynching site. During the lynching, groceries were scattered along the river bank. Among the groceries were slabs of fat pork, which later rotted on the river bank because the dogs and other animals in the area refused to eat the meat.

Many of the residents in Walton County felt that they knew who was included in the lynch mob. It was alleged that many of these included local law enforcement officers from Walton County. Blacks were employed as maids for some of the alleged suspects, and they recounted episodes of death bed confessions, and horrific death experiences on the part of the suspects. One lady told of one of the suspects, before he died, not being able to stay in a room without the shades being drawn and lights out. Even with this, he would often scream out "get the N---- off of me."

Although this event took place sixty-one years ago and is still under investigation, no arrests or convictions have ever been made. Residents of Walton County and surrounding areas are still reluctant to discuss this event.

ഌ‍ഌ

Summer vacation;

A quaint cottage on the lake,

Feels like paradise.
                              -M.T. Knight

The Gladiators
Therry N. Deal

Our American homes have become the coliseum
The windows arch up, or the windows are square
THE BATTLE IS FOR OUR MIND

Inside we are the spectators at a hundred battles performed
before us by the medium of TV
THE BATTLE IS FOR OUR MIND

We take our seats, often with snacks in hand,
perhaps our hasty supper
The entire family comes to and fro
The children may have their own seats in
the corner of the bedroom
THE BATTLE IS FOR OUR MIND

The protagonists may vary
politics
soaps
music
advertisements
All have their ideas
THE BATTLE IS FOR OUR MIND

THE LIGHTS GO OUT

Thanksgiving Memory and Perspective of Same

Evangeline Lundy

Have you ever experienced a mixture of conflicting emotions? Joy mixed with sadness? Happiness mixed with a degree of fear of the unknown? Have you ever built a new home and moved into it before it was completely finished, on the day before Thanksgiving? We did.

The moving date was non-negotiable because of the contract agreement. We had lots of rain a few days before and during the day of the move. The electricity was turned on the day before, which allowed us to have hot water and to have the electric range for cooking. Our "soon to be made beautiful home" had sub-flooring in 90% of the house. The bricklayers were still in process of laying brick for outside walls. We had a real wood burning fireplace, our very first one.

On Thanksgiving day we woke to misty rain. I made breakfast and started to unpack the kitchen boxes. My husband and son went outside to cut wood from some of the trees that had to be cut down. After working for hours, I made a quick lunch and called to husband and son to come in out of the bad weather. They came in and built a fire in the fireplace, using the wet wood. We were anxious to see if the fireplace would "draw" properly and provide heat. The scent of the wet wood burning was pungent and strong.

The fireplace, however, appeared to be working properly and we were cheered and warmed by the flames. Our nine-year-old son said to me, "Mother, where is the turkey?" I said, "Oh, we aren't having one today," since I could not find our utensils to make our usual Thanksgiving dinner. His expression changed from pleasant to sad. "We wlll have one for Christmas as we will have everything ready to use in a few weeks."

After lunch they went back outside to work at cutting the wood. Darkness came early, and they came inside. I made sandwiches for us and we went to bed early as we were completely exhausted from our moving chores. We had moved across town and had enrolled our son in a new elementary school.

Eventually we had a finished, beautiful new home. We made friends with our new neighbors and we moved our church letter to a church in the community. Toward the end of school year, I was going through our son's school papers, determining which papers to keep and which could be thrown away. I picked up a paper that had a title at top of the page that said, "My Thanksgiving Day."

> We woke up to see that it was raining and cold.
> After breakfast Daddy and I went outside to
> chop wood for firewood.
> We chopped wood all morning. Mother called
> us into the house for lunch. We had hot dogs
> for lunch.
> We made a fire and got really warm and dry.
> Then we put on our coats and Daddy and I
> went back outside to chop some more wood.
> When it got dark we went inside and had
> sandwiches for supper and went to bed and
> that was my Thanksgiving Day.

Tears quickly sprang to my eyes. Every word that he wrote was true. This was the experience from his PERSPECTIVE. From my perspective I was overjoyed to be in our new house, and unpacking and preparing to make this new house a comfortable home for us. Suddenly the contrast of our two perspectives struck me as irony and I started to laugh. I kept the letter and showed it to my husband. We both felt empathy for him having had an unexpected kind of Thanksgiving Day.

I told my husband that it is a wonder that someone at school did not bring us a basket of food as the impression was given that we were in need of it. I went to see his teacher and took the letter with me. She was very kind, and she understood and appreciated the circumstances that had prompted his paper describing his Thanksgiving Day. We never told our son until years later about this experience. By that time he, too, was able to appreciate the irony of the situation.

Perspective is everything. What is actually true and how that truth is expressed can be just the opposite from another perspective or point of view. Since that day, I have in all the years since never failed to personally prepare the turkey and dressing and all the trimmings for our little family on Thanksgiving Day.

Epiphany of Spring
Ethelene Dyer Jones

Look, the winter is past; the rains are over and gone.
Blossoms appear through all the land.
The time has come to sing; the cooing of doves is heard in our land.
-Song of Solomon 2:11-12 (NCV)

The trees pregnant now with new-formed buds
Respond to rising sap and warming sun.
Blue skies with cumulus clouds like foaming suds
Help Nature wash away the winter dun.

A gentle March wind stirs the fallen leaves
And hints of springtime flow in songs of birds.
For deaths of friends my heart now sorely grieves,
But soon comfort and healing will be stirred.

Cycles of Nature move on expected rounds
Through winter, spring, then summer days and fall.
Life, too, leads us through unknown grounds
Of seasons—dark and light—all with a pall.

Hope rises as on wings to lift and cheer;
And faith, a close companion of winged hope,
Forbids any season to unload such abject fear
Or dispense darkness so dense one cannot cope.

Just as the boughs are ready for spring birth,
So we, cloaked well in hope, can cancel strife,
Look up, find beauty in the breadth and girth
Of all the signs of resurrection and new life.

The Trip of My Dreams (Why I Love to Travel)
Margaret Knight

I must confess, there is a great joy that I feel in the discovery of new people and different places. Although this was my third trip to Europe, I had seemingly waited a thousand years to take the trip of my dreams. And now, my dream was finally a reality.

Every trip is always pregnant with possibilities. This one would be no different. There would be people to meet, new adventures to experience, and perhaps a new me to discover.

It is difficult to explain, but when I set out on a journey, I feel a newfound freedom, a liberation of spirit and a willingness to experience the emergence of new friendships.

During this trip, we met people that we shared taxis with; we experimented with food dishes more esteemed by the local people than by my esophagus. By the time our vacation ended, we had met people who we posed with for photos, exchanged addresses, and pledged to keep in touch. Ultimately, we may or may not see each other again, but the interlude remains vivid and intense in my mind.

Travel is as much about who we are as where we are. Once there, we cannot help but see ourselves as others see us. In Lyon, France, my sister, Edie, and I boarded a train headed for Perpignan in the South of France. It was a six-hour train ride. When we reached our compartment, there was a young Frenchman already seated inside. We smiled and greeted him in French, using our limited proficiency in the language. We were drawn to his warm and incandescent smile. He was eager to practice his commendable conversational English, and we found ourselves, for the next four hours, talking incessantly about California, Georgia, French cuisine, about racism in France, French and U.S. politics, religion, history and more. By the time we reached his destination at Montpellier, four hours later, we were best of friends. I extended my hand to him in friendship and farewell, but instead, received a big bear hug from him. He then removed a small container from his pocket and placed it in my hand. It was very touching. All three of us hastily exchanged email addresses and he quickly left the compartment and exited the train. A few minutes later, he was outside our window, trying to get our attention while waving goodbye.

As the train pulled away from the station, I opened my hand to inspect the small container he had placed there. It was a small, round tin with the words "Cachou Lajaunie," written in French. I opened the small container and discovered what appeared to be minute, black charcoal pillars which were strangely familiar to me. I put one in my mouth and immediately was taken back to my childhood days when my father used to carry these in his pocket and gave them to us for treats. He called them "sin-sin" and he used them as breath fresheners. What an experience!

Travel encourages exploration and invites new experiences. In Amsterdam, I learned how tolerant people were. There, the diversity of human beings is an understatement. It is incredible how so many different races, religions, sexual preferences and ethnicities can co-exist harmoniously in one place.

The tolerance goes even farther. We went to the famous Floating Flower Market in Amsterdam. There we saw seeds and plants of every variety, from Mums to Marijuana. We were surprised to see Marijuana seeds and plants being sold, legally. Not only were the seeds being sold, some were already planted in little containers where all one had to do was add water and watch it grow.

Another example of tolerance was the fact that sex is not taboo in Amsterdam. Even the television commercials contain nudity and it's no big deal. Neither is the vast number of openly gay in Amsterdam. We later discovered that Amsterdam is the gay capitol of the world.

Mark Twain once wrote: "Travel is fatal to bigotry, prejudice and narrow-mindedness."

For me, travel has been the education that I could never have achieved in school. Travel has been my best teacher of geography, history, art, humanities, languages, and foreign currency, just to name a few.

Ultimately, travel has encouraged me to include the world—its conflicts and its celebrations—in my thinking. When world events happen, whether devastating typhoons, civil unrest, terrorist bombings, or world sporting events, they somehow connect me in a vivid and instinctive way because I've been there, I know the people, I remember. Sometimes, even the movies I see which are filmed in locations in different parts of the world, somehow connect me, perhaps, because I have been there. I recently watched a movie that was filmed on location in Venice, Italy. I connected, vividly, because I had been there. I remembered.

In the years ahead, I pray that my health and physical stamina, as well as the condition of my wallet, will allow me to continue to travel and be adventurous. And even if my wallet is a little lighter on my return home, I will surely be satisfied that my photo albums will be much heavier.

Perhaps the best travel lesson that I have learned through the years is that the world is much smaller than I ever imagined—and there are some hearts that are much larger.

This article was originally written on September 1, 2001, after my return home from Europe. Ten days later, terrorists destroyed the World Trade Center in New York. Because of the unrest in the world and the inconvenience of traveling due to the increased security measures involved, my love for travel has been dampened in the years that followed 9-11.

After the 9-11 attack, the young Frenchman whom my sister and I met on the train in Lyon, France, emailed me the most sympathetic and touching letter. He told me that as he was typing the email, the president of France, Jacque Sherac, was making a speech on their national television with deepest condolences from the French people for the disaster that had befallen us here in the United States.

ೞೞ

Please remember me
As someone who loved music,
And sweet muscadines.
                    -M.T. Knight

Against the Odds
Irwin Gates

I was dead and am alive. During my office visit with Dr. Richard Harvey, he sat back with a disconcerting smile on his face. He was obviously pleased to see me. He told me that of all people who have ruptured left ventricles 90% die without making it to the hospital. Of the 10% who do make it to the operating room, only half leave the hospital alive. I was pleased to join this minority group. The doctor and I both knew that it was more than medical skill that contributed to my continued life. There were more people praying for me than I could have imagined. The Fellowship Class, members of the church I attend, the Northeast Georgia Presbytery personnel, members of other churches, groups of which I am a member, friends, relatives, and even some people I don't know. When people say it is a miracle that I survived, it makes me feel uncomfortable. Why would God allow me to live and 95% of those who have a ruptured left ventricle die? I don't know. All I know is that God goes with us in every experience of life.

It all started out simple enough. In October 2000, I went to Dr. R. John Barrett, Jr. with the complaint of pain in my shoulders and neck. He referred me to physical therapy at the Oconee Regional Medical Center. I was given a series of exercises involving my arms and shoulders. This gave some relief, but I continued to have pain. From my readings as a Rehabilitation Counselor, I knew that sometimes pain in the extremities can signal a heart condition. The next time I saw Dr. Barrett I requested a stress test. I had been exercising four or five days a week for seven years. I expected the test to be a walk in the park. I had been taking Pravachol, one of the statin drugs, because my HDL cholesterol was low. Dr. Barrett put ten heart leads around my chest and I started walking the treadmill. Before I got started well, Dr. Barrett shut the treadmill down and called a heart specialist in Macon. He put a nitroglycerin patch on me, gave me a pill, and asked me to report to the Medical Center of Central Georgia for a heart catheterization the next day. Dr. Zoe J. Jones did a heart catheterization with a post-procedure diagnosis: "Needs by-pass surgery." There were vein blockages of 50%, 70%, and 90% of the blood supply to my heart.

On December 26th I had triple by-pass heart surgery performed by Drs. Randy Brown and Richard Harvey. The surgery went well and I seemed to be recovering. However, two days later my blood pressure dropped. Dr. Mark Dorogy was visiting the Intensive Car Unit and asked the nurse how I was doing. The nurse indicated that I was doing well and they were about to transfer me to a regular hospital room. He said, "I don't think so." He could see that my feet were elevated above my head. He gave cardiovascular pulmonary resuscitation. Of the possibilities of what might be wrong, bleeding after the operation was the most likely. He contacted Drs. Brown and Harvey. An operating room was available and they took me back and opened me up again. There was a small leak in the left ventricle, which burst just as they got me open. They clamped it off and repaired the ruptured left ventricle and the damage it had caused. They put in another by-pass, giving me a quadrilateral by-pass. I was carried to recovery and later returned to the Intensive Care Unit. After the operation, I had tubes coming out all over my body. There was an IV which I was receiving, a tube up my nose to feed me, a ball pump to regulate a fluctuating blood pressure, a catheterization tube, two stomach drainage tubes, and a ventilator in my mouth. Apparently, few of my bodily functions were working on their own.

My wife tells me that I was kept in a drug-induced coma so that I wouldn't move around and tear apart the second operation. When I came to myself, I was transferred to a regular hospital room on another floor. They had my legs in support hose and had put some inflated boots on my feet because I was rubbing my heels on the bed trying to push myself up in the slanted bed. Soon they had me up and walking and I was discharged.

The recovery was going well until I started having difficulty breathing. I called Dr. Barrett, who had me go to the emergency room at Oconee Regional Medical Center. While I was in the emergency room, my chest opened and infection started draining out. Dr. Virgilio Valdecanas took me to surgery and cleaned up the area. I was transferred to the Middle Georgia Hospital. As it turned out, I had staph infection. I had to be cut open again to have my ribs debrided, cutting off the dead bone. The bone apparently died because of the lack of blood supply. I had plastic surgery which Dr. Howard Perofsky performed by cutting my pectoral muscles and attaching them to the debrided bone to give blood supply. When I shared this fact with Lovett Briggs later, he said "You don't look any better." The process took care of the infected area, but it did not take care of the staph infection. I was referred to Dr. Quyen Luu, an infection control specialist, for treatment of the staph infection. She placed me on strong IV antibiotics for about a week in the hospital and for forty days after leaving. I had home health service give me the IV at home for forty days.

This adventure gave me a deeper understanding of the Church Universal. Those who prayed for me were from many different churches and groups. Is this not the Church? People call my living through this heart attack a miracle. It was. The mystery of living through a ruptured left heart ventricle, in which 95% of the people die, still bothers me. Does God have some purpose for my living? If He does, what is that purpose? I wish I could answer these ponderings with certainty, but I have to leave them as mystery. I can respond with certainty that God goes with us in every experience of life; God is the first to be there.

Times
Patricia Byrd

There are times in life
When we grow
And times when we wait.

There are times when strife
Is all we know
And times that are great.

Death at Times Is Kind
Ethelene Dyer Jones

How can I rue your death and cry and weep?
Why keep holding on as if to delay
Your grand entrance to Heaven at the gate
That leads to peace and everlasting life?

We shared a faith that keeps in life and death
A steadfast hope for better times beyond.
How could I deny the crown awaiting you
And all the joys of labors finished here?

As I beheld your earthly face aglow
With life's last smile, a halo to recall,
I knew that wishing you a longer stay
Would be denying you your golden shore.

Death at times is kind, good, a blessed release;
It brings us into quiet, enduring peace.

෫ඞ෬

Ripples on water

Like bright sparkling diamonds,

Reflect the sunlight.
                    -M.T. *Knight*

To Begin Again
Barry Darugar

After forty years of studying English, I am still overwhelmed by the cadences and nuances of my adopted language. I wonder: How am I going to balance myself on the precipice while stepping off into a whole new world of communication without totally breaking all that ties me to my native tongue and traditions, all that defines my identity?

I studied the English language for several years before receiving a scholarship to study in the United States. To master English, as with any second language, requires years of immersion in the culture as well as in its literature.

I started my internship at Louisville General Hospital in January 1960. Shortly afterwards I was called to start an IV on a young girl. She was about 5 feet 5 inches tall, 190 pounds. I diligently tried to start her IV, but I could not find her small veins. After several attempts I said, "You are fat. I can't find your vein." I noticed a startled look on the nurse's face, and the young girl started crying. I gathered something had gone wrong, so I left saying, "I am sorry." My explanation that calling someone fat in Iran was not a derogatory remark did not prevent Nurse Pritchard from calling me an insensitive Middle Eastern chauvinistic pig. In that era, before the Iranian revolution of 1978, few people had heard of Iran and generally my homeland was referred to as a Middle Eastern country. Even fewer people knew about Iran's six-thousand-years of history, civilization, and dynasty.

During my internship year from 1960 to 1961, every morning I usually gave a brief presentation of my patients' history and laboratory findings during morning visits of our professor.

Dean Kumin, one of the senior residents, was a thin, tall man with crooked yellow teeth from smoking and reddish-brown, crew cut hair. He would shout like a drill sergeant, "God-dammit, you are supposed to be here at 6:30 a.m. It is already 6:45. How are you going to be ready for the morning presentation?"

I would have liked to say, "I didn't get out of the hospital until 7:30 last night, I hardly had time to eat and get some sleep," but he interrupted my thoughts. "Get your ass in gear," he ordered.

After the rounds, he cussed another intern out. The intern's presentation caused cancellation of Kumin's thyroidectomy. Dean could have burned a hole into that poor intern's face. "If you ever cause me to lose another case, I'll ride your ass all the way back to the Philippines," he said. The intern was a Philippino.

In that era, abuse of cheap labor, interns and residents was common. We worked forty-eight hours straight, then twelve hours off, but in actuality we never got off on time. We had barely time enough to introduce ourselves to our estranged family and get a few hours of sleep before going back to work. No wonder we were chronically tired, our wives were depressed, and our children were maladjusted. Our salary was about one hundred dollars a month which was not even enough to buy groceries. To pay the rent, utilities, and clothing we had to borrow. As a tired, poor intern I had no time to learn ethical language or social graces from interaction with a higher echelon of people, so I used what I learned on the job, including profanities. Unfortunately, I used my new vocabulary in the wrong places and among strangers. I was called to the administrator's office.

"Kouros, I hear you're using some colorful profanities," he said.

"I am not sure what you mean sir, but I know my language skills are not up to par."

"Patients and staff are complaining about your use of G.D., shit, and F words."

"I thought they were solid expressions used by doctors to make their point," I answered.

After a short interview with me and hearing my explanation, the C.E.O. realized my naiveté and kindly advised me to refrain from using slang words that I did not exactly understand. After over thirty years of living in the United States, I am still learning the nuances and intricacies of the English language. The English language, like Farsi and Arabic, has a very rich heritage. So many words have similar meanings on the surface but the essences of them differ greatly. For example, skinny or thin versus slim or trim; obese or fat versus plump or healthy, chubby versus stout, ambitious versus avaricious. Some of these words, such as "ambitious," have a different connotation among Americans versus British. In some other words, like "impotent" versus "impudent," a slight mispronunciation can totally change the meaning. To understand the underlying connotation of referring to a woman as "an alley cat" versus "a fox" requires more than just casual studying of the language. For me the process was a gradual transformation. I heard language in English first, translated it in my brain to Farsi, tried to digest it, then translated it back to English. The problem is that Farsi is written from right to left, an adjective comes after a noun, but in English adjectives come before nouns: a good man = *mard-eh-khoob* (man a good) in Farsi. Similarly, in Farsi adverbs come before verbs, in English after. *Aâ hestah Mee Ravad*, slowly walks he.

I initially dreamed in Farsi but as the years passed I started to dream in English and Farsi both without going through translation. Now I primarily dream, speak, and think English, but consciously or in my dreams I can speak Farsi if it is necessary. This process of transformation in my speech and thinking patterns saddens me. The fading of the Persian culture and language that was imprinted on my subconscious is inevitable. The childhood memories, the poems that I memorized and the literary prowess that I possessed lost their clarity and luster. Writing out my memoir is in part an attempt to recapture, rejuvenate, and preserve my identity.

Not long before my departure from Iran I started a diary, mostly about my love life and my excitement and fear of leaving familiar settings for unknown territories. I continued to write my diary in Farsi for several years. But recently I realized that if I am going to write about my life, it needs to be about what I am now – an American; however, I also need to preserve and write about who I was and where I came from. My American self becomes oddly more objective. What I was is a perception that only exists in the abstract of my memories and also perhaps in the sphere of thoughts and observations of others.

Early in my career I realized that speaking the English language correctly and without an accent would be a crucial tool in my advancement. Most immigrants can overcome their marginality and the presumption of lower status in the rural south by uttering correct sounds and pronunciations. I thought "Yes, speech is a class signifier." In the rural south of the late sixties, the blacks and foreigners, when compared to natives, were like Southerners measured next to the Yankees. They were viewed as a notch or two below the inner sanctum of the intellectuals.

I envisioned that I stood on a precipice where I either had to balance myself or fall into an abyss of anonymity. The adrenaline secreted because of this fear pushed me to competitiveness. I had a choice: I could let my status as an immigrant restrict me, or I could confront the challenges with spunk and optimism. These twin influences of fear and ambition have persuaded me throughout my adult life. Nowadays, facing similar challenges, I say, "Been there, done that."

***

While I was at Emory I met a prominent Persian family who had migrated to the United States with a good bit of their wealth, just before the revolution of 1979. Syrus, their eldest son, while in Tabriz, controlled a large group of farm workers. "I had total charge of three villages. More than two thousand peasants were working for me. No one dared to touch me, even though it was common knowledge that I was a supporter of the Shah," he boasted.

"Why did you leave Iran?"

"Ayatollah ordered seizure of my belongings and declared me a *Kaufir* just like Salmon Rushdie," he replied.

"Did you have a price on your head?" I asked.

"No! I wasn't big enough, but since I was condemned to death by Ayatollah it was every Moslem's duty to slay me."

He went on and on about his life-style in Iran and how he was going to remain true to his heritage. He insisted on speaking Farsi and adhering to some of the impractical traditions of the old culture such as having more than one wife, using ewer after having a BM, and expecting his workers to obey him unconditionally. He talked about his many disappointments and the various problems that he was facing.

"You need to adjust to the American society," I said.

Nostalgia is a pregnancy of memories, all that we have left behind —the way we were. If the labor pain of longing and remembering ever culminates in the delivery and riddance of the nostalgic notions it might actually, for some like Syrus, symbolize an abandonment of what they have been made of—their heritage.

***

I endured the hardships of medical training: humiliation, chronic fatigue, poverty, and hunger. I tasted the bitter taste of rejection from one residency program and experienced the joy of acceptance in an even more prestigious institution.

Surgical training decades ago was in the form of a pyramidal system. In the second year of training at Emory, sixteen residents were accepted, but by the end of the third year only eight residents advanced. By the end of the fourth year only four residents were promoted to Chief Residency. The others, who did not advance, either went to other specialties or transferred to other programs. The competition for the top position was intense and the anxiety associated with it was immense. I was summoned to Dr. J.D. Martin's office, the chairman of the Surgery Department at Emory University. Dr. Richard Amerson, vice-chairman, and my favorite professor, was also present. I was shaking inside. My knees were weak and my mouth dry. I forced myself to walk in and sit in one of the chairs. I had already heard rumors that one of our senior residents was not promoted and another one was transferred to urology. I wondered if I was the next one to get axed. We all worked hard. Everyone of the residents was a smart and dedicated physician. Who would be the chosen one? None of us had any clues.

Dr. Martin said, "I am looking at your dossier. You came here highly recommended—top of your class and a member of the honor society—but you knew in advance that our program would eliminate fifty percent of the residents during training." My heart skipped a beat and my chest tightened as if in a vise. "Do you feel you have developed your skills and shown the enthusiasm, dedication, and judgment that is required of a top notch surgeon?"

"I have done my best, sir."

"Let us see what your peers and professors have to say about you in the last three years." Dr. Martin and Dr. Amerson reviewed my file.

My heart thumped rapidly and the sweat ran down my armpit. It seemed like an hour even though it was only a few minutes before Dr. Amerson said, "I have worked closely with Kouros and he is a meticulous surgeon."

Dr. Martin smiled, picked a few pages out of my file and said, "Everyone gives you high marks. They laud your dedication, enthusiasm, skill, and judgment." Then he looked at Dr. Amerson and asked him, "What is your recommendation?"

"I feel he should be promoted."

Dr. Martin stood up and offered his hand. "Congratulations. You are one of our four chief residents."

I was elated beyond description. I walked out as if walking on clouds. I whistled "Oh, Happy Days" all the way back.

***

My development in American society had an immense effect on me and my family. The pangs of anxiety and fear etched their marks on all of us. The tragic loss of my first wife and other defeats and disappointments left their scars on my children as well as myself. I felt like a wandering Greek navigating the depths of Hades. I sought the blessing of forgetfulness and desired not to remember much.

The process of assimilation was particularly difficult for me. In classrooms I nodded to indicate I was following the lecturer when I did not understand. My brain could not translate the spoken English quickly enough. I listened to jokes, but did not find them funny. I pretended to laugh with others even though I did not get the punch line. I felt alienated. I wanted to be in the inner circle but I was also apprehensive of exposing my inadequacies. I questioned who I was. As if a ghost of my previous self, I tried not to occupy too much space. After all, with a sense of disadvantage and inferiority I could not feel large-hearted enough to be generous to myself.

Years later, enrolled in the creative writing program, I am bewildered again. My mentors tell me, "Find your own voice."

"I don't know how to find it," I say.

I read and imitate from myriad styles, too many to choose from. I am different from most other students. Perhaps, the denouement of what "my voice" is and my success in finding it lies in my otherness. The uniqueness of my voice may resonate from my original point of view askew as it may be.

It took years to pick apart and digest the babel of American language, to apprehend its wit and style. It will take even more years of reading and writing creatively before the nuances and cadences of English snap smartly into the synapses of my brain so that I can generate melodious and lyrical lines that will electrify and titillate the senses of my readers. For now at least I can laugh at the joke about the five-hundred-pound canary.

Eclipse
Mal and Sandy Mallinson

It was noon in Mysore, India…
The "Golden Bird" bus stopped.
"All out," the driver shouted in Indian.
"What in the world is happening?" we asked.
"Eclipse!" was the answer.

As we stepped off the tourist bus, we saw that we were at a hotel, and most of the bus passengers and driver had disappeared into the hotel, terrified of the eclipse. We knew that an eclipse of the sun was due that day; it had been in all the newspapers, including the dire effects of being caught outdoors during the darkness: sickness or death could result; food left out had to be destroyed; even animals had to be washed to remove the harmful effects of the eclipse.

We lingered, then decided to walk into town but found the streets empty and stores closed and fastened tight. Turning back, we found a lovely park where we could observe the celestial phenomenon. Already a hush and greenish tinge surrounded us—the eclipse had started.

I pulled a notebook out of my pocket, tore out two pages, with a pencil punched a hole in the center of each, and we held them up toward the sun to let the image fall onto another page. A crescent showed—the eclipse! We looked up to find a group of young people in their late teens gathered around us, staring. One fellow (the only one who could speak English) asked, "What are you doing?" I explained, and he translated to the group.

"Then is there no danger in being out in the eclipse?" he asked.

"No, the eclipse is not magic; it is a natural happening." And we gave them each a paper with a hole to see the crescent for themselves. Oohs, aahs, nods, questions, answers. One young man ran off and brought back a newspaper that explained with a diagram how an eclipse worked.

A man sleeping on a bench nearby was awakened by the eager voices. Someone said, "Eclipse," and he jumped up and took off running.

We were standing near a tree, and one observant fellow cried out, "Look!"

There on the ground were crescents formed from the sun shining thru the leaves.

What an occasion! About twenty young Indian boys and one shy girl all eager to learn. As the excise approached the end, the group walked with us to the hotel. The young spokesman said to me, "They wanted me to tell you 'Thank you' for teaching us about the eclipse." Then the young people went inside the hotel, gathered the fearful adults, brought them outside and demonstrated to them what an eclipse was.

Now we knew they had learned!

ട്രാൽ

Christmas Decorations

Doyle Boyd

The house was well decorated

As you can see...

From the coffee table manger scene

To the overly decorated Christmas tree.

Stanley as a girl!

Why I Am Not a Boy:
A lesson in Behavior Modification
Martha Chandler Tomlin

Growing up as a little girl in a household with three brothers, 7, 10, and 12 years older, can be hazardous to your mental health! According to my mother and my Aunt Mary Lizzie, I was often a toy for them to tease. At mealtimes, my brothers liked to amuse themselves by having me try to pronounce big words, sometimes naughty, which I did not understand the meaning. While we shared a mutual affection, sometime in my early years I began to feel the worst horror that could happen to me would be for me to become a boy. I refused to wear a pair of overalls from my daddy's store so I could look like my brothers. After all, my mother was an excellent seamstress. She enjoyed making pretty dresses for her long awaited little girl.

About the same period in my early life when I developed an aversion to my brothers, I acquired the unladylike habit of "kicking up my heels." Although rebuked by Mother, I continued the habit of lying on the floor and kicking high enough to show my panties—sometimes before visiting company. My favorite spot for exercising was under the kitchen table while Mother was cooking.

One eventful day my oldest brother, Stanley, who was 12 years my senior, taught me a lesson in what would be described today as behavior modification. I was under the kitchen table enjoying my antics and was being observed by Stanley. He leaned over to tell me that once he had been a little girl like me, but he had kicked up his heels and this had turned him into a boy!

Seeing that I was doubting his story, Stanley took me to his room to show me a picture of himself. Sure enough, on his bureau was a picture of him dressed in a long frilly dress and standing in a wicker chair. He solemnly explained this was a picture when he was a girl. Kicking up his heels had turned him into a boy.

I was convinced. From that day forward, a stern look from Mother, coupled with a warning from a teenage brother, helped teach me to be a lady.

I still think it's great to be a girl!

Someone Gave You Flowers
Margaret Ann Daniel

"Someone gave you flowers," the nurse said to the figure who lay swathed in white bandages on the bed.

There was no response. There was only mute staring up at the ceiling with blue, blue, crystal-blue eyes.

The nurse bustled around, her starched white uniform rustling slightly as she placed the flowers at the foot of the bed and cranked the bed up so that the vacant eyes could look at them. Leastways, the flowers were in the line of sight, if there was a sight.

She finished her bustling and left, shutting the door behind her.

She was back out in the wide antiseptic hall now, pushing her flower-laden mercy cart.

She pushed open a second door and carried in a profusion of nosegays tied with a pink silk ribbon.

An old lady sat at attention in a chair by a window, her knotted hands folded in her lap, her spine straight, her feet flat on the floor, the picture of dowager elegance of a bygone era.

"Someone has sent you flowers!" the nurse said, with a quasi-surprised tone in her voice.

The old lady did not speak, but merely nodded a curt acknowledgement.

"Let's see, where shall I put them, dear? Oh, I know! I'll set them here on the bureau, so they're reflected in the mirror and it will look as if you have two identical bouquets. Isn't that clever of me?"

The old lady looked her own haughty look in the nurse's direction.

"I'll be going now. Bye bye, dear!"

She gave a little wave as she backed out the door, almost backing into her cart.

She had lined the flowers up precisely to coincide with the doors of their recipients, so as to heighten her efficiency. Really, she would have liked to arrange them artistically on the cart, but to what end? Better to put efficiency over beauty, she always said.

Her next stop was the room of a forlorn child. This little girl's flowers were special, all tied up in a little bouquet and set down in a tea cup, the mate of another tea cup and a teapot in which previous blooms had appeared. The child sat up in the bed and clapped her hands when the nurse entered.

"See, honey, someone gave you flowers!" She added the tea cup bouquet to the other tea set pieces which were accumulating on the lovely little tray that had been filled with pansies on the day she delivered it.

"We'll have tea, you'll see," she said to the little girl.

The child gave her special nurse a smile of heartbreaking trust.

And so the nurse went about her duties until the end of her day, when her feet were swollen and she could walk only far enough to rest at the bus stop on her way to her evening job.

In her room above the flower shop, she counted her money and estimated how long it would be before she could afford more beautiful flowers for her special patients. Then she went down to work in the coolness of the flower shop, where the owner let her work to help defray the expense of the flowers.

$$\mathcal{SO}\mathcal{CR}$$

Happy dogs playing
On freshly mown green grass lawn,
Having lots of fun.
                    -M.T. Knight

Spider Lilies
Mary B. Purcell

Previously published:
Mary Binnicker Purcell, "Spider Lilies," *The Peacock's Feet*, Vol. 23, (1998) 20.

I don't know how

you do it every year,

timing your entrance

like a debutant

at her "coming-out" ball,

casting her eyes about,

making sure that

all the others are

dressed in their drab

browns and grays.

You stand,

your slender body

poised and elegant,

laughing at the wind,

who is whispering secrets

while his hands are

rustling your ruby red hair.

Choices
Susan Lindsley

Because the robin always loved the sunset colors best
The colors of the sunset now adorn the robin's breast.

The mockingbird loved music more than flowers of the spring,
So now he sings the songs that all the other birds can sing.

The meadow lark is also marked by something he likes best—
The lines of fences zagging through the golden fields out west.

Avoiding chores of motherhood the cowbird thought was best,
So she will always lay her eggs in someone else's nest.

Because he feels a little shame in seeking out the dead,
The buzzard floats forever with his blushing on his head.

Eagles saw the mountains standing tall against the sky
And thought that over mountains was the perfect place to fly.

Oh, you can spend your lifetime singing like the mockingbirds,
While everything you say just echoes someone else's words.

Or you can be a buzzard, you can scavenge from the air
Or always sit on fences, never going anywhere.

Or you can build a nest upon a rainbow in the sky
And sail the music in your heart to where the eagles fly.

There'll Be Some Changes Made – Today
Jan Williams

My mom, at the age of 65, made a drastic change in her life. She left her home in a small west Georgia town and moved to the big city of Atlanta into a retirement home for senior adults. She made this decision without consulting another soul.

I was living in the suburbs of Atlanta with my husband and two teenage boys. Her sister, Stella, was living in Atlanta not too far from this complex. It seems that on one of her frequent visits to the city she had met some ladies who lived there and they began to tell her what a nice place it was. Well, the seed was planted! Later she came to spend the weekend with us and dropped the bomb-shell. "I am moving to Atlanta," she said. Speechless was not the word to describe my reaction —shell-shocked would be more accurate. I began quizzing her on this decision. You know the regular questions—are you sure about this? Have you checked it out thoroughly?

"Yes," she said, "I have checked it out, and I have made my decision. My name is on the list for the next available apartment. I should know something in about two weeks. Now, Janice, you must not tell my brothers and sisters. I want it to be a surprise." That would turn out to be the understatement since four brothers and one sister lived within ten miles of her.

"When exactly do you plan to tell them?"

"When I get the call that the apartment is ready, I will call the moving company to schedule the date. When that is confirmed, I will call them the day before I am to move."

Is that "gutsy" or what!

"Why are you waiting until the day before you are to move?"

With this devilish look on her face, she said, "Because they will try to talk me out of it, but it won't happen. I'm ready for the sidewalks and street lights in the big city."

It happened just as she had predicted. Her siblings did have a few (hundred) words as to why she should not move to Atlanta, but she stood her ground. My phone rang with frantic voices at the other end of the line questioning my mother's mental state. I assured them that I was as shocked as they were. My only explanation was "mid-life crazies."

Here I must tell you WHY I did not think this was a good idea for her to come to the big city. Previously, when she wanted to come to Atlanta for the weekend, she would drive to my aunt's house, leave her car, and I would shuttle her either to my house or to her sister's house in

Atlanta. She was also afraid of many things: driving in traffic, being alone, new situations—and that is just for starters. I knew my life was about to change also, and I didn't think it would be for the better.

Nonetheless, Bob and I met her with the moving van to help her get settled. "Do you need to go anywhere, Mother?" I asked "Like to the drug store, grocery store, bank, etc.?"

"Well, maybe just to the grocery store for a few things."

After stocking her pantry, making the bed, putting away the boxes and making sure all the papers were signed, we said it was time for us to go. I really thought she would ask me to stay the night with her.

No way was that about to happen. She was singing, humming, whistling. She was a totally different person. We had not seen this side of my mother. We were happy and sad at the same time for the growing pains that come with any move.

"When you have finished with the grunt work, feel free to leave," chirped my mother.

And we did—ENJOY, MOM, WE LOVE YA!

Soft summer breezes
Like the breath of an angel,
Brush against my cheek.
                    -*M.T. Knight*

The Fishing Trip
Mary Binnicker Purcell

I don't even have to close my eyes. Right this minute, I see the early morning shadows hiding in the moss-covered trees as my daddy and I slip noiselessly along the black water's mirrored surface at Devil's Elbow on the brackish waters of the Augustine Creek. As the sun spreads her fingers of light out into the darkness feeling for the day, our leaky boat, loaded with sharpened hooks, a lamp, matches, string, and grasshoppers, glides along the water. As Daddy paddles, I begin to set the bush-hooks with the grasshoppers Daddy and I had captured the night before from the tall dog fennel weeds, and the lines are tied to the bushes and brush hanging low over the water.

I can hear my daddy, "Just let his feet touch the water. That's right. Let the grasshopper dance for our breakfast."

After the bush-hooks are all set, Daddy paddles back to our starting point on the creek where those first lines are taut; the fish and turtle are dragging the bait and hook as each tries to escape. But my knots will hold. I am confident in my ability; I have done this hundreds of times before, and we know that the occasional splash up ahead will put smiles on our faces—and meat on our table.

Summer Vacation
Geloria Phelps

During the summer I used to go on vacation with my mother and sisters. We always went on the last Sunday in July, immediately after church services. The trip originated in Atlanta with my mother and two older sisters. Then they would stop in Winder to pick up my baby sister, and then to Milledgeville to get me.

We traveled down 441 South until we reached Dublin, where we would get gas before getting on I-16. We always had plenty of snack foods with us, including pound cake, cheese straws, carrot sticks, and low-cal dips. You see, my baby sister was always on a diet. She would be the driver because she thought she knew more about Savannah than the rest of us. Being the youngest, she always wanted to have her way. We would get to Savannah about first dark and would find our way to Abercorn Street to find a hotel.

Since we never made hotel reservations, we frequently stayed in some hotel that might be described as "seedy." This is why we always traveled with a can of "Off." Monday morning would find us up bright and early and ready for the first day of our vacation. One reason for our early rising was that my baby sister would start her "Morning Meditation" at 5:30 a.m. She would read her Bible and then commence to sing hymns in a loud voice. My older sister, who was always the sleepy head in the family, would roll over and look at the rest of us and say, "I wish she would shut-up, so we can get some sleep." The rest of us agreed silently. However, this did not deter my baby sister. She continued to sing as she showered and dressed. Then she would go right into her morning exercises. One of her favorite exercises was the "side-straddle hop." She would count one, two, clap, one, two clap. By this time the rest of us were furious with her. We would get up and get ready for the day.

My mother was ninety years old, but she never missed a beat. We would argue over where we would have breakfast and recount the breakfast experiences that we had in the past. One time everyone in the party ordered a buffet breakfast, all except the "Dieter." She would steal food off our plates, until she was "busted" by the waitress, who noticed that she had a small plate filled with breakfast items. When we finished breakfast, we checked out all the stores in several strip malls in the area. Next, we headed out to Tybee Island for the rest of the day.

When we arrived at Tybee, we would go in different directions. Those who liked the feel of sand between their toes would head for the beach along with my mother. She always wanted to get to the beach and put her feet into the water to help her arthritis. She swore that the ocean water was the best thing she could find for her arthritis, and after all, who would argue with Mother Nature. The rest of us, who did not want sand in our shoes but just wanted to see the beach sea gulls, would head for the Pavilion. While the beach combers roamed the beach, the Pavilion crowd sneaked off to the concession stand to purchase hot dogs, even though it was a bit hard to cover up the onion breath. Finally, we went to the little shops on Tybee to purchase souvenirs for our husbands. We always bought baseball caps with the word Tybee written on the front; after all, we had to have evidence that we actually went to Tybee.

At the end of the day, we always stopped at Williams Seafood for dinner. They had delicious seafood and served generous portions. Then we went down to the waterfront; you see, the dieter always had to get some pecan pralines to carry home with her. One time we were sitting down on the water front when we were officially welcomed to Savannah. A sea gull flew over our heads and left a signature on my sister's shoulder. She jumped up screaming, "He got me!" and demonstrated by using her hands to show how the sea gull flew away. We stayed down on the waterfront until late in the night. "Mother Nature" would take a few short (sitting) naps between events.

One time when we left the waterfront, we had to find our way back to the hotel in the dark. We ended up on one of the many squares in the city and could not seem to find our way around those squares. The squares were hard enough to navigate in the daytime, and even harder at night. We went around and around the squares. Finally, my mother, who was napping in the back seat, woke up and discovered that we were having a little problem. She looked out of the window for a while, as we continued riding around and around. After a few more trips around the square, she said, "We have been around this sign that says Bull Street about five times. This is making me dizzy."

We all started laughing. We finally found our way off the square.

My sisters and I have continued taking our yearly vacations in Savannah, though they are not the same. Our mother passed away in 2001. Her spirit remains with us, for we continue to include her tradition as part of our vacation. I can still see her with her feet in the water each time we visit Tybee Island, and we always chuckle when we see the sign that reads "Bull Street."

My First Best Friend and My Beloved Quilt
Martha Chandler Tomlin

During childhood my best friend was Anne Lawrence. I cannot recall the exact time we became best friends. Our parents lived near each other in the Browns Crossing community. Her father, Roland Lawrence, was Governor Eugene Talmadge's appointee to head the Men's Prison on Highway 22 leading into Milledgeville. "Miss" Dollie, Anne's mother, and my mother went together to enroll us in first grade at Peabody Elementary.

According to our teacher, Anne and I were never far apart at school. We were quite opposite in looks. Anne had jet black hair; I was a true blond. However, both of us had Buster Brown hair style and detested having our bangs cut.

What made us best friends? We sat together during our 15 mile school bus ride morning and afternoon. Both of us were chatterboxes which got us in trouble. For example, in first grade, Anne and I often had to be separated and rest on our work tables to keep us from talking to classmates who rested on nap rugs on the floor. We always wanted to be on the same team at recess playtime and we shared our lunches prepared by our mothers.

Most students were dismissed at lunch time. Because Anne and I were "bus kids," we had to wait to ride the bus until GMC students were dismissed. At this time, GSCW (now Georgia College and State University) focused on graduating future teachers. Those of us riding the bus were supervised after school by a practice teacher. After completing our homework, we could play on the playground. Anne and I loved the swings and would swing high enough to cause the chains to jerk, after which we competed on jumping the longest distance from the swing.

Anne and I loved to spend the night with each other. We played the card game of Hearts, pick-up-sticks, jacks, jump rope and hop-scotch on our paved walk. We played school, alternating being pupil and teacher. At mealtime our favorite pastime was giggling—not eating. We only had to look at each other to go into spasms of giggling. Even with Mother's scolding, there were many giggles before dessert. One of the best things about being best friends was our birthdays. We could spend the night with each other, exchange gifts and celebrate with our families.

In the winter of fourth grade, Anne was hospitalized with pneumonia. The first night after she returned home, mother took me to see her. We did not visit long, for Ann seemed too quiet. Before leaving, Anne wanted to give me a gift. I told her goodbye and went home with two large pearl beads (possibly pearl buttons) and Anne's Big Little Orphan Annie comics. This was to be our last visit. The following morning mother came to my bed to tell me Anne had died during the night.

This was my first experience with death. I cannot remember if my classmates and I were at the funeral. As one classmate recently said, "We loved her." I had lost my best friend and I missed school for the next two days.

After Anne's death "Miss" Dollie contributed books to Peabody Library in Anne's memory. For me, she made a copy of her only picture of Anne seated at a child's table when she was 3 or 4; the wooden frame was made by an inmate at the Men's prison.

Through my 18th birthday, "Miss" Dollie would always remember me with a gift. Among them are six silver tea spoons of different patterns.

My Special Quilt
Martha Chandler Tomlin

My mother liked to quilt. "Aunt" Mary Johnson, a member of Brown's Crossing black community, would come to our house and would sit on the low pea-shelling chair with a basket of cotton beside her. With much skill, she would fashion a stack of soft batting by using the batting cards which I still have.

Mother liked to do her quilting during the winter months. The quilt top, with lining and batting between, would be suspended from the ceiling on a frame made by my father. The frame would be lowered to chair level and the sides could be rolled inward as her tiny stitches progressed. After mother finished her sewing sessions, the frame would be raised to the ceiling.

During her lifetime, Mother made a special quilt for each of her children. Mine was the last of four. It is very special. The pattern is Martha Washington's Flower Garden; I share my birthday with George. With the exception of one square (contributed by Aunt Laura), it is made entirely from scraps from Anne's dresses and mine during the school years we had together.

This beautiful quilt has remained on the foot of my bed for many years for me to remember a special friendship.

Adversity
Ethelene Dyer Jones

Prosperity is not without many fears and distastes;
and adversity is not without comforts and hopes.
                              -Francis Bacon (1561-1626)

Adversity often stalks in the wings,
threatening to come on stage
and steal the show, give the cast
new lines and new scenes.

Adversity, dressed in tribulation,
can bring vexation and cares,
turn one aside from purposes,
leave a grievous aftermath.

But what is this through dark shadows—
"adversity is not without comforts and hopes"?
What can be learned in adversity's camp
that is hidden when the sun is brightest?

There are ways—and ways—to go;
one is beset with pitfalls, another a detour
around which boulders of doubt
must be met and dealt with head-on.

In retrospect we will be able to see
that adversity had its purpose
to make us stronger, to grow us
into responsibility and purpose.

Therein are the aspects of adversity
that make life's road change direction,
help us access the avenue of hope,
lead us up mountains to comfort.

                              August 6, 2007

Author Biographies

Doyle Boyd was born in Mississippi. After several years of moving to different locations, he decided to settle down in Milledgeville, Georgia. He is married, has four children and seven grandchildren. He earned a B. A. degree from Mississippi College in Clinton, Mississippi. He also earned a Master of Science degree in social work from Florida State University in Tallahassee, Florida. He has practiced professional social work in Milledgeville since the early 1970s.

Patricia S. Byrd is married, has two children and three grandchildren. She writes poetry and prose for pleasure. Ms. Byrd is a member of the Georgia Poetry Society and Georgia Freelance Writers' Association. She has a Bachelor of Arts degree from Mercer University and a Master of Science degree from GCSU. She is a member of LIR Writers and hopes to publish a novel one day.

Ed Bzdyk was born and raised on Long Island, New York. As a young man, he was a member of the United States Air Force, at which time he wrote a short story and won second prize in a base-wide contest. He has also written a number of short vignettes revolving around childhood experiences. He is married to Norma Jean, a registered nurse, has four sons and eleven grandchildren. Ed served as President of LIR and participated in the LIR writing group while living in Milledgeville. He presently resides in Shoemakersville, PA.

Carrie Cox was born in Baldwin County, Georgia to the late Bill and Annie George. She was married to the late Jack Cox and has six children, 13 grandchildren, and eight great-grandchildren. She has two sisters, **Marie Horton** of Milledgeville and Anne McCollum of Macon, Georgia. Carrie enjoys writing and is interested in helping her fellow writing friends in the L-I-R Writer's Group.

Margaret Ann Daniel returned in 2005 to Milledgeville, Georgia, her home town, after retiring from the Fireman's Fund Insurance Company, where she worked for many years in Greensboro, North Carolina and Atlanta, Georgia. She contributes the *Milledgeville Memories* column to the <u>Baldwin Bulletin</u>. She is preparing a collection of her columns for publication.

Barry Darugar is a retired general and vascular surgeon. He was born in Iran and graduated Summa Cum Laude from Teheran University. He received a scholarship to further his studies in the United States of America. After a year and a half at the University of Louisville, Kentucky, he transferred to Emory University where he completed his studies as a surgeon and became a diplomat of American College of Surgeons in 1966. He practiced medicine and surgery from 1965 to 2002 and also held the position of Clinical Assistant Professor of Surgery at Mercer University in Georgia. After retiring, he completed the undergraduate courses in creative writing and entered the MFA program at GCSU where he has now completed the requirements of this degree. He lives with his wife Debbie and a Maltese dog named Nikoo on Lake Oconee. His four children and five grandchildren all live within one hundred miles of his home. Several of his articles and poems have been published in various national journals such as Medical Economic, Touchstone KS, Colere IA, World Order, and also locally in Peacock's Feet at GCSU. He is also the 2004 first place nonfiction award winner at GCSU. He has written a book of memoirs titled *Out Of Iran* and is in process of writing his second book.

Harriet Davis recently retired from Central State Hospital as supervisor of Neurology and Cardiology. She is widowed with three children, Jannell, Jacobi, and Anthony, and six grandchildren. Wanting for many years to become a motivational speaker, eight years ago she joined Toastmasters. She not only learned to deliver speeches, but she found out that she also had a love for writing short stories. Her stories range from serious subjects to her favorite, tall tales (embellishing the truth).

Therry Dawne Nash Deal was born in North Carolina in the country on a farm. Her undergraduate degree was from Woman's College of North Carolina. Therry received her Ph.D. in Human Development from the University of North Carolina at Greensboro. Part of her doctoral program was completed at Harvard University. She has served on the faculties of the University of North Carolina at Greensboro, The University of Georgia, and as a Dean at Georgia College and State University. Following her retirement, she completed the Education for Ministry Certificate from the University of the South. She and her husband, J. B., have two children and four grandchildren. Although Therry has been a widow for 16 years, she is active in professional organizations, civic organizations, and has been elected president of one national professional organization. As her parting administrative gift to Georgia College, she created the Learning-in-Retirement program.

Irwin Gates is an honorably retired ordained minister who was ordained over fifty years ago. He served churches in Lockhart, Aiken and Greenwood, South Carolina as well as Sandersville and Wayside, Georgia. He worked as a Vocational Rehabilitation Counselor for the State of Georgia. Irwin received Clinical Pastoral Education under Anton Boisen and later under John Crow. He was married to his first wife, Charlotte Cox, for forty-eight years. They had three children: James, Peter and Grace Anne and three grandchildren. Irwin is currently married to Gladys Turner. They reside in Milledgeville, Georgia. He enjoys traveling, dancing, bowling, and kayaking. He wrote about his heart condition because it is rare for a person to survive such an experience.

Sandra J. Jasnau is from Canada. She is married to Ken Jasnau and they have four children and five grandchildren. She and Ken are active members of the Baha'i Faith. Sandra was educated at Ryerson Institute of Technology in Toronto, Ontario, Canada. Her interests include knitting, crocheting, water color painting, and weaving tapestry for wall hangings; the cover of *Milledgeville Tapestry* is a piece Sandra produced.

Ethelene Dyer Jones grew up on a farm in Union County, GA. She lived most of her life in the North Georgia Mountains, becoming a resident of Milledgeville, GA in February, 2003. Married to the Rev. Grover D. Jones, she enjoyed being a minister's wife, the mother of two children, seven grandchildren, and two great grandchildren (to date). She is a retired educator. She received degrees from these colleges: Truett McConnell (AA), Mercer University (BA), Western Carolina University (MA), and the University of Georgia (SEd). She is the author of two published books of poems, three books of history, and has written for several newspapers and magazines. A book of county and local history which she compiled and edited, *Facets of Fannin: A History of Fannin County, Georgia,* is now in its seventh printing. She was a presenter at the Georgia Literary Festival held in Blue Ridge, GA September 28-30, 2007.

Margaret T. Knight is a retired Federal Administrator and was Field Office Manager for the Social Security Administration in the San Francisco Region. She graduated from the University of California at Los Angeles (U.C.L.A.), and the California State University, Northridge.

She received a Bachelor of Science (BS) Degree in Public Health Administration, and a Masters (MPA) Degree in Public Administration. Her writing won her First Place at the 2006 Southeastern Writers Conference Award For Juvenile Writing.

Susan Lindsley, a Milledgeville native, wrote for pleasure even after writing became her profession. She wrote news and feature articles for The Macon News; she edited the first papers on the laser and on telemetry, and wrote the handbook used to eradicate smallpox. Her fiction, nonfiction and poetry have won literary awards. She has three published books, two of poetry and one nonfiction entitled **Yesterplace: Blue Jeans and Pantaloons in Post World War II Georgia**, which recounts the fun and pain of life on a Baldwin County "plantation."

Evangeline Lundy graduated from the University of Georgia with a B.S. degree in Consumer and Family Finance and a minor in Journalism. While there she met her husband-to-be in a chemistry class. The chemistry must have been right as it lasted for 51 years before his death in 2001. She has lived in eight different towns in Georgia because of promotions and transfers of her husband, but she has been on Lake Sinclair in Milledgeville longer than any other place. Evangeline has been an instructor at Wesleyan College and a high school teacher in Macon. She retired from Georgia Power Company with 27 years service. A charter member of Learning In Retirement, she enjoys Reading Club, Writing Class, attending Edlerhostels and travel. A son, daughter-in-law, and one granddaughter are "the wind beneath her wings" and encourage her in all her adventures into what life may offer.

The team of Howatt E. and Minnie H. Mallinson (alias Mal & Sandy) has been sailing along ever since their wedding in 1946. He was born and brought up in Queens Village, N.Y., while she was across the ocean in Xuzhou, China, but they met in Atlanta while he was at Georgia Tech in the Navy. He became a pastor, while she taught school and then went into nursing. They raised their five children in Virginia and North Carolina, then traveled with backpacks around the world and taught in China and Taiwan. They currently live on Lake Oconee near Eatonton, GA. And the grands and greatgrands keep coming.

Geloria Ansley Phelps was born and raised in Barrow County, along with one brother and four sisters. She resides in Milledgeville, is married, and enjoys reading and writing about growing up in a small rural community in northeast Georgia called Tanner Bridge.

Mary Binnicker Purcell is retired after thirty years with the U.S. Postal Service. Upon retirement, she worked for several years teaching English and journalism. She is married to Jim, and they have two children and four grandchildren. Mary is from Savannah, Georgia, but has lived in Milledgeville, Georgia, for over thirty years. Her interests include writing, theatre, and law. She received her Bachelor's of Science degree (1998) and her Bachelor's of Arts degree (2003) from Georgia College & State University. She is an award-winning writer and teaches writing for Learning-In-Retirement sponsored by GCSU in Milledgeville, Georgia.

Shane Riner – son of Mark and Jeannie Riner of McIntyre, Georgia, is a home-schooled 16 year-old with an interest in writing, skating, and video games. He doesn't know what his life work will be, but he hopes to write and to work with computers.

Martha Chandler Tomlin was born February 22, 1924, in Baldwin County in the community of Brown's Crossing. Her parents farmed and operated Chandler's store, and a cotton gin. She attended Peabody Elementary and High School, graduated from Mercer University with a B.A. in English and received her Master's degree in Social Work from Tulane University. Martha has enjoyed a career in various fields of social work in Louisiana, Mississippi and Georgia. After her retirement from Central State Hospital in 1990, she enjoyed classes in music, American and English history, and women's studies at GCSU. She has served as organist and pianist for several Milledgeville churches. In 1999, Martha lost her vision to macular degeneration. With the help of two low-vision friends, she founded a support group for the visually impaired. Now that Martha no longer drives, she is spending time writing her memoirs. Martha has four children and a granddaughter.

Margaret Anderson Uhler is a native of Florida and has lived in Milledgeville, Georgia, for nearly sixty years. She was a part-time English instructor at Georgia College & State University for twenty years and is the author of The Floridians.

Jan Williams lives in Eatonton, Georgia, with her husband Bob. They moved to Eatonton from Ormond Beach, Florida, where Jan retired from a real estate career after 25 years. She and Bob have two married sons and four grandchildren. Jan has been involved in storytelling for many years. She is a natural—with most of her stories built around family members. Jan doesn't hesitate to compose a drama with just a few facts, and her humorous stories help others to see how easy it is to laugh at the ordinary patterns of living.

Martha J. Williams was born in Alabama, but has lived most of her adult life in Milledgeville, Georgia. She has spent her career in education, first as a teacher, and later as an administrator. She is an alumna of Georgia Military College, Georgia College, University of Georgia, and South Carolina State University. She is married to a former teacher, has one son, and five grandchildren. Her hobbies include reading, writing, and traveling.